SUPERB WRITING
TO FIRE THE IMAGINATION

Kathryn Cave writes: 'This story takes place in the no-man's-land where real life and fantasy meet. That's where I bumped into Septimus Similon one winter afternoon many years ago. He had wandered out of Stolk Castle with his head full of theorems and lost his way. I've seen him many times since then – on a moonlit platform as the last train to Ongar drew in; racing frantically after a number 10 bus; late night grocery shopping in Camden Town; stepping out of a lift. I scarcely have time to register who he is before he's gone. Over the years I've become rather fond of him.

Sep is a true wizard, fascinated by ideas to an extent that makes him a highly dangerous person. In this story he embarks on an ingenious experiment which turns out to have awesome real-life consequences. Among those he inconveniences are his helpers, Kevin and Alison, and his more or less terrifying colleagues. It took me two years to write their story and although I was often inclined to tell the lot of them to frog off, I made it in the end.

I hope you enjoy this edition, with its wonderful illustrations by Chris Riddell.'

Also published in Hodder Silver

The Lammas Field
Catherine Fisher

The Brugan
Stephen Moore

Omega Seven
Maggie Pearson

The Burning
Judy Allen

Sunwing
Kenneth Oppel

Mirror Mirror
Louise Cooper

Law of the Wolf Tower
Tanith Lee

SEPTIMUS SIMILON,
Practising Wizard

Kathryn Cave
Illustrated by Chris Riddell

Hodder
Children's
Books

a division of Hodder Headline Limited

For Joe

A Catalogue record for this book is available from
the British Library

ISBN 0 340 77850 4

Typeset by Avon Dataset Ltd, Bidford-on-Avon, Warks

Printed and bound in Great Britain by
The Guernsey Press Co. Ltd, Guernsey, Channel Isles

Hodder Children's Books
a division of Hodder Headline Limited
338 Euston Road
London NW1 3BH

Chapter One

Someone stole Alison Braythwayte's schoolbag from her locker. It contained thirty-one pence, her bus pass, and a whole term's history notes.

'It can't have gone!' She closed the locker door and opened it again in a hopeful way. 'It was here after lunch when I got my physics books.'

'Well, it's not there now,' Janice said. 'Are you sure you didn't take it to the lab?'

'Of course I'm sure!' The full extent of the disaster slowly dawned on Alison. 'What am I going to do without my notes? There's a test on Friday – that's tomorrow. I've got to revise tonight.'

'Tell Mr Dempsey,' Janice suggested.

'The Head?' Janice was much given to off-the-wall suggestions, but this one struck Alison as worse than most. 'I suppose he's going to find my history notes for me?'

'No. But he's always saying how every problem has a solution, isn't he?'

That was quite true. Alison nodded.

'So let him find a solution to this one, then. If he hasn't gone home, that is.'

What did Alison have to lose? She set off at top speed along 200 metres of corridors, raced down one flight of stairs and up two more flights, and pounded on the staffroom door.

Mr Dempsey had gone home. So had Miss Grice, the history teacher.

'What am I going to do?' Alison said in despair.

'I'd lend you my notes,' Janice said generously, 'if I didn't need them.'

'I'll have to borrow them from someone else!'

Janice shook her head. 'Most of them have gone by now. And if they haven't, they'll want their notes themselves – you know what Miss Grice is like. It won't be easy.'

Easy? It wasn't even *possible*.

'Look, I'm sorry and everything, but I can't stay,' Janice said half an hour later. By then they were in the senior cloakroom. Alison was looking desperate and resolute, refusing to give up. 'Everyone's gone, and I've got to meet Pug from his piano lesson at four-thirty. Mum doesn't let him out after dark.'

'Someone's still here. Look!' Alison pointed to the far side of the cloakroom. A dingy brown parka dangled on a hook by the door. In a flash Alison was up and darting across to it.

Janice followed. 'Yuck! Whose is it? Is there a nametape?'

Shaking her head, Alison plunged a hand into one pocket. 'No, but this feels like a ticket or something – yes! Oh!' Her voice fell. 'It's a library card for someone called Kevin Young.'

'Who?' Janice asked blankly. 'Is he in our year?'

'No – Yes! I've heard the name,' Alison said, racking her brains. 'I think he came at the beginning of term, when they closed Greenhill.'

'There you are, then!' Janice began to button her coat. 'Look, I've got to rush or I'll be late. See you tomorrow.'

Along with the library card, Kevin Young's pocket contained a ballpoint pen, two fluffy Polo mints and a letter from the library demanding the return of four overdue books.

Alison turned the letter over and wrote on the back:

Please will you lend me your history notes tonight? I am *desperate*.
Signed: Alison Braythwayte
(38 Field End Road. Tel: 254559)

She speared the note on the peg above the parka and began the long walk home through the December drizzle.

In his attic room at 38 Field End Road, Septimus Similon (practising wizard, fourth class) checked and rechecked his calculations. If they were correct, he was going to surprise a good many people.

He thought the calculations were correct.

He felt they were correct.

By his pounding heart, by his trembling fingers as he turned the pages of the books that lay six or seven deep on every surface of his attic bedroom, he *knew* they were correct.

After fifteen years of dry and tedious study, he, Septimus Similon was about to make history.

The calculations covered the back of two supermarket receipts, a chocolate wrapper, and a demand to S. Similon for the immediate payment of library fines. Twice Similon lost his place and had to begin again.

In the world outside, dogs barked, car horns sounded, aeroplanes thundered – Similon didn't raise his head. Two floors below, the telephone rang and rang unanswered. Finally, as day drained away, footsteps approached along the pavement and halted outside number thirty-eight. The door-bell rang and, when no one responded, the unseen caller pounded on the door.

'Similon!' a voice cried through the letterbox. 'Similon, you cloth-eared nincompoop, are you there?'

Deaf to everything outside the attic, Similon hummed as he unrolled a map on top of the piles of books on his table. He took a pair of compasses from the old shoe he used as a desk-tidy, and stuck the point into one particular spot on the map. Very carefully, he drew a circle.

The hammering on the door stopped. In the sudden quiet, feet could be heard quite clearly descending the steps. On the pavement outside number thirty-eight they hesitated and then moved off, gathering speed.

As his visitor accelerated into the darkness, Similon whistled a small tune of triumph and switched on the light.

In the cloakroom at Westleigh High, Kevin Young peered at the note. He hadn't a clue who Alison Braythwayte was but it seemed to him there was just the glimmer of a possibility that the whole thing

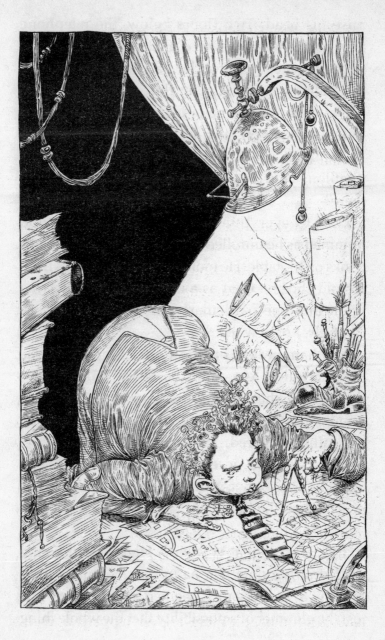

wasn't a joke. He looked at his watch.

Four fifty-five.

Too late to get to the library before it closed.

Field End Road wasn't that far, and he had his bike.

You can't get a note and just ignore it.

Kevin called home to say he'd be late and pedalled off.

By the time Alison reached home, the drizzle had turned to rain. Her hair hung in rat's-tails. She dropped the key on the doorstep, fumbled it into the lock with numb fingers, and bullied the door open. She was in urgent need of hot chocolate, several slices of bread and honey, and a lot of sympathy.

Unfortunately, the tall, narrow house was empty, if you didn't count their lodger (and Alison certainly didn't). Sep was in all right: she could hear him creaking back and forth, two floors up. But there was no Mum (working late, again), no Dad (for the past four years), and in all probability no chocolate powder, bread or honey either. Alison unbuttoned her sodden coat, releasing a flurry of drips on to the pile of mail that lay on the doormat.

She stooped and picked the envelopes up.

No letters for Miss A. Braythwayte from her throng of admirers. No real letters at all, just bills and junk mail, plus the big envelope that came each month for their lodger. For months after Sep arrived with one tiny suitcase and twenty-eight staggeringly heavy boxes (each of which Alison had helped haul up to the attic), she had hoped the weekly envelope might have something exciting inside: secret instructions, possibly, or at least a hefty cheque. It was a blow to hear from her mother over breakfast one morning that it was only some course Sep was taking – maths or Latin. Something foreign, her mother had said, all signs and theorems. Alison had lost interest in both the envelope and Sep from that moment.

That afternoon, however, there was nothing else remotely interesting in the mail, and Alison gave Sep's envelope a thorough inspection. Whoever had typed it had obviously been in a hurry: the letters were higgledy-piggledy, and some of them had disappeared completely:

eptimu imilon
38 Field End Road
Axborough
Middl ex
England
THE OTHER WORLD

Ha-ha, Alison thought sourly, reaching the last line. Very funny.

8

In the top left corner there was a scrawl in purple. The light in the hall was too dim to decipher it by, so Alison took the envelope into the sitting-room and switched on the lamp.

Hmm.

The sender was apparently someone by the name of Ungerl or Urgert.

Field End Road wasn't where Kevin thought it was.

That was all right. He hadn't expected it would be.

He pedalled along through the gloom peering at street names, undiscouraged.

The circle was drawn, the calculations complete. All that remained was to carry out a final check on wind speed and direction.

Similon unfastened the window. Before it banged shut again, a flurry of icy rain flung itself into his face.

Good. The wind was still north by northwest, as it was supposed to be.

It was time to assemble the constituents within the circle on the map.

Earth. Plenty of that on the sole of his shoes. He stamped his foot, picked a pinch of dried mud off the carpet and placed it inside the circle.

Air. The room was full of it.

Water. A raindrop would do. He dipped one finger into a splash on the windowsill and wiped it gently on the circle.

Fire. This bit always made Similon nervous, but it had to be done. He took a match from the box in his slipper, struck it, and held it above the mud and the raindrop.

Downstairs the telephone rang and was answered. Up in the attic Similon heard nothing but the hiss of the match and the thud of his own heart as he began the final incantation.

'Braythwayte here,' Alison said crisply.

The line emitted a ferocious crackle. 'Tell that idiot No,' said a far-off voice. 'It's dangerous. Warn him!'

Alison held the receiver away from her head, looked at it hard, and then replaced it gingerly against her ear.

'To whom do you wish to speak?'

The line crackled again. 'There's no frogging time!' the voice shouted. 'Hurry or it'll be too late! Go now! Run!'

Alison had no intention of being one of those people who go to pieces in a crisis. She took a deep breath and said calmly, 'You're in some kind of trouble, aren't you? Tell me where you are and I'll ring the police.'

'*I'm* not in trouble, it's *him*!' Another burst of crackling, more deafening than before, and then the voice shrieked, 'Tell Similon. Tell him No!'

Similon? The message was for Sep?

'No what?' she shrieked back.

In a sudden lull, the voice said quite distinctly, 'Logios thirty-ni-i-i-ne!'

'This is a joke, isn't it?' Alison said crossly. 'You're one of Sep's friends, I bet. You didn't fool me, you know. Ha jolly ha.'

If there was a reply, the crackling swallowed it.

There was a click and the line went dead.

Kevin was at a crossroads within striking distance of Alison's house when the lights went out. All of them: streetlights and houses.

'Power cut,' he told himself knowledgeably. 'I went left last time, so this time I'll go right. I'm almost sure it's this way.'

The beam of his bicycle lamp wobbled gamely on into the night.

Alison stood in the dark clutching the telephone. To her irritation, her heart was working overtime. 'It's just a stupid joke,' she said again stoutly. 'And the light needs a new bulb.'

Two floors up, the attic floorboards creaked. The noise made the house seem emptier than ever.

Without thinking, she groped for the telephone and dialled her mother's office. Her mother never minded being rung at work. Maybe she wouldn't be in a meeting. Maybe she could come home early after all, and inform Sep, kindly but firmly, that hoax telephone calls were no laughing matter.

No ringing tone. Alison put down the telephone and lifted it again.

There was no dialling tone either.

Friends . . .? a voice inside Alison's head asked. What friends? Sep didn't have friends, he was too droopy – droopy and boring. Nobody ever rang him up or came round to see him. The only letters he got were the brown envelopes once a month.

With a start, Alison remembered the latest envelope, still on the windowsill where she'd dropped it when the phone rang.

Could the purple scribble on the front really have said Ungerl? Maybe it was Ungert? Urgert?

Alison gasped as inspiration hit her. Not Ungerl or Urgert . . . Urgent!

What had the voice on the telephone shouted?

'Tell him No!' Alison whispered. 'Run!'

Up two flights of sixteen stairs, two at a time, Alison ran.

Chapter Two

There was something strange about Webber Street.

It looked normal enough, but as Kevin passed the fifth house, something sprang up from the tarmac just ahead of his front wheel.

He braked and fell off.

When he picked himself up, he turned the bike so that the lamp shone straight ahead. A small goat stared back at him with yellow eyes. There was snow on its back.

When Kevin stepped towards it, he found himself walking backwards.

The moon swam out from behind the clouds and revealed a dense forest, staggering close, rank upon rank of tree-tops silhouetted against the sky. A distant howl rose eerily into the night.

Not distant enough.

Kevin turned his bike and pedalled furiously back the way he had come.

A faint light glimmered beneath Sep's door.

Alison hammered on the door. 'Sep! I've got a letter for you. It's urgent!'

'Hang on.' He sounded out of breath. 'Something's happened to the lights. I've found a candle, but it keeps dripping. Ow! It did it again. Have you brought a spare bulb?'

'It's not the bulb, it's a power cut.' Alison beat a brisk tattoo on the door. 'Open up, Sep! Someone rang for you too. I've got a message.'

'Hang on,' he said again. 'I'm going to wind a sock round the bottom of the candle. It can drip on that. Right!' The door opened and the Braythwaytes' lodger appeared. To Alison's relief, apart from the sock-wrapped candle, he looked the same as always.

'You're all right!' she said. An expression of surprise appeared on Sep's mild, boring face. She hurried on, 'This person rang for you, you see—'

'For me?' Sep's straggly eyebrows rose, making

him look like an astonished sheep. 'Well, well, that was quick. How did they get your number? I don't even know it myself.'

'Never mind that,' she said impatiently. 'What matters is the message. They told me to tell you not to do something. It's dangerous.'

Astonishment gave way to mild anxiety. 'What's dangerous?'

'Whatever it is they don't want you to do.'

'That's not much good,' he said reasonably enough. 'If it's dangerous, I don't want to do it either. But I can't not do it if I don't know what it is. Are you sure it was me they wanted?'

'They said your name: Septimus Similon. Maybe it was some kind of joke.' Alison shivered. She was beginning to recover and was suddenly conscious that the top landing had no radiator. 'Look, it's freezing out here. Can't I come in?'

Similon was standing in the doorway. He retreated, closing the door to a crack. 'Can it wait? The room's a bit of a mess. The vacuum cleaner isn't working. I can't find a duster. I was going to tidy up tomorrow. Hey!'

With one firm push on the door, Alison was past him and into the attic. 'I don't mind if it's untidy, Sep – Oh!'

Her first impression was books, wall to wall and floor to ceiling. Books on the bed, the carpet, the windowsill, the table. Books festooned with hundreds of torn strips acting as bookmarks, interleaved with sheets of paper bearing Sep's spidery handwriting, crisscrossed with crossings out.

'It's not as bad as it looks.' He kicked the nearest book under the bed. An enormous black cat emerged and stared at them balefully, before leaping on to Similon's table and sitting down on the map.

'Is that yours?' Alison asked, stunned. 'You're not supposed to keep a cat up here!'

'It's not mine, it just lives here. Don't tell your mother.' Similon looked anxiously at Alison. 'I've had a lot on my mind. You know how it is. But that's all over now. I've finished. I'll straighten things up first thing. Clean sheets, tidying, dusting. I'll empty the wastepaper basket, the whole thing.' His face became thoughtful. 'I'll have to clear up soon anyway. There'll be people coming, once the news gets out. They'll probably want photographs.'

Alison dragged her attention away from what looked like a mouse's tail marking a place in the book at her feet. 'What news? What have you finished?' A disquieting thought struck her. 'Not what the person on the phone was going on about, I hope?'

'No, no,' Similon said soothingly. 'All I've done

is refute Logios 39.' Alison jumped. 'Technically it's rather tricky, and no one has actually managed it before. In fact, so far as I know, no one has ever disproved any theorem of Logios until now. But it isn't dangerous. It's of purely theoretical interest.'

'I hope you're right,' said Alison.

Beyond Park Road lay the common, so-called; a patch of turf where people walked their dogs morning and night. Beyond that was the dual carriageway, crowded every night with commuters returning home. Beyond that lay Glebe Gardens, where Kevin lived. The only problem was that when Kevin reached Park Road, the dual carriageway wasn't there. Instead of the stream of car lights and the roar of traffic there was silence and night.

Kevin dismounted and wheeled his bike across the grass towards the place where the underpass ought to be.

There was a yelp from not far ahead. A dog raced out of the darkness and streaked past Kevin, ears flattened, tail between its legs, lead trailing.

The owner followed moments later. For an elderly man, he was making very good speed.

Once again Kevin turned his bike and pedalled back the way he had come.

Alison settled herself comfortably on a stack of

books. 'So what *is* this theorem you're all excited about, Sep?'

'Logios 39,' he answered. 'I told you. I've had a hunch for months that I could disprove it. For the past week I've been almost certain. And now –' he beamed, 'I've done it. You can't imagine what that means to me. It's all very well to have a diploma to say you're a qualified wizard, but what does it prove?'

Alison fell off the pile of books. 'I beg your pardon? Did you say "wizard"?'

'That's right. You know how long it took me?'

Dumbly she shook her head.

'Fifteen years.' He ran his fingers through his hair. 'Do you know how many theorems I had to memorise?'

She shook her head again.

'Seven hundred and seventy-seven. And the practicals!' He rolled his eyes. 'You'd think at the end of all that – well, you'd think I'd really know something, wouldn't you?'

Alison nodded. She was still in shock. Sep didn't look mad, or no madder than normal.

'But I *didn't*! Take my thesis: I must have spent all of two years trying to prove Logios 15 was true. I mean, sometimes I could make it work, and sometimes I couldn't. The wind would shift, upsetting everything. I kept running out of frogs.'

'Frogs?' Alison's voice was husky, but Similon swept on.

'And to really prove it, to be absolutely *sure* it was true, I'd have had to make it work in every conceivable set of circumstances. I'd have had to spend the rest of my life proving it! So then I had my brainwave!'

Alison looked towards the door. It seemed a very long way. She cleared her throat. 'And what was this brainwave?'

'It's simple when you think about it. Even if a theorem works a hundred times, you can't be sure it's true. But if you can make it *not* work even once, then it's *not* true. And if you know it's not true, you know something. So I stopped trying to prove Logios was right, and I started trying to prove he was wrong. And the other wizards looked at me as if I was mad, and Fentwick – he's my supervisor – didn't turn up for tutorials, and I wrote to Amalik of Pinner and Corilex of Gerrard's Cross, and they never wrote back. I don't mind telling you, I was within this much of giving up and going home—' Similon's voice shook with emotion.

'Where's home?' Alison asked, against her better judgement.

'Back in Theromantia. I can't remember exactly. That was why I didn't go, really. And now it's all worked out for the best. Because I've done it!'

The cat rose to its feet and gave a low growl.

'Ah! It wants to go out,' Similon said. He opened the window and the cat vanished into the darkness.

'Where were we? Oh yes, I was explaining about Logios 39. Basically, what it says is—'

Enough was enough. Alison rose from her pile of books. 'Er, yes. Well, that's very interesting, Sep,' she said carefully. 'Thank you for telling me. I'll just pop downstairs and find you a new bulb. Be back in a minute. Be careful with that candle, won't you?'

'I haven't finished yet,' Similon said plaintively. 'In fact, that's just the beginning. According to Logios 39 . . .'

A short exchange of ritual significance was in progress at the far end of Field End Road.

'Terrible is the wrath of the enchanters.' The speaker broke off to sneeze. 'Sorry, it's this newting weather. Terrible is the wrath of the enchanters and righteous their – their—'

'Revenges,' his fellow agent said testily. 'Hurry up. I want to get home. Skip a bit. Dreadful are their something or others and whatever happens to Septimus Similon, it serves him jolly well right. Amen.'

'Amen!'

'What's the address again?'

'Number thirty-eight.'

'Come on. And the council says, Remember Chesterfield. No witnesses this time.'

His partner sneezed again. 'No living witnesses.'

'Come *on!*'

They moved on down the road.

The hammering on the door started while Alison was feeling her way down the stairs.

'All right!' she called from the first landing. 'No need to break the door down. I'm coming!'

But when she reached the hall, certain warnings about not opening it to strangers popped up in her mind. It seemed all the more important to take care with Sep apparently entirely off his rocker. Suppose the hoax caller had their address as well as their telephone number? Suppose he was out there, on the doorstep . . .

'Who is it?' she called sternly through the letterbox.

'Me!' came the answer. 'I got your message. It's me, Kevin! Look!'

Alison recoiled as the middle section of a face appeared centimetres from her own, on the other side of the letterbox. 'Don't you recognise me?' its owner asked anxiously. 'I've got my Travelcard. Look!' For an instant one section of Kevin's face was replaced by a London Transport identity card. A pair of brown eyes peered hopefully at her above the plastic.

'I'd have got here sooner but there's been a massive power cut. Everything's pitch-black. I had to use my bicycle lamp to read the house numbers. Can I come in?'

The lamp settled it. With light she could find candles and matches. Ten seconds later, Kevin was inside. Ten minutes after that, he was sitting opposite Alison in the sitting-room, listening to the story of the hoax caller and Similon's plunge into madness, while the candles flickered.

When Alison had finished, he cleared his throat. 'And the phones don't work?' She shook her head. 'Have you got one of those radios that runs on batteries?'

'Yes!' Alison jumped up. 'In the kitchen. Wait a minute.'

'Because if it's a really big power cut, it could be on the news.'

Alison was back already, radio in hand. 'And even if it's not on the news, it'll give us something to listen to while we think what to do – oh, bother!' She dropped the radio on to the sofa in exasperation. 'It's not working either. And I only put new batteries in on Sunday.'

'Ah.' Kevin cleared his throat again. After a pause he said, 'Spooky.'

'It's not spooky,' she responded crossly. 'I probably left it switched on. There's a perfectly

22

ordinary explanation for everything. There's been a power cut, Sep's gone mad, and I forgot to switch off my radio. It's not spooky, it's just really, *really* annoying. I'm never going to get my history revision done now.'

'Sorry.'

There was another pause during which Alison glared and Kevin stared down at his hands with a furrowed brow. Finally he cleared his throat again. 'Did he say what this theorem was that he'd disproved?'

'Not really. He just said it was Logios 39. The person on the telephone said the same.'

'Logios,' Kevin said in a knowledgeable voice. 'Logios, eh?'

'Who is he, for crying out loud?' Alison demanded.

'Search me,' he said, surprised. 'He probably made the name up, didn't he? If he's mad and all that.'

Alison frowned. 'I don't think he did,' she said, surprising herself. 'When I was up in the attic, he used two big books to wedge the candle. I think it said *Logios Volume 9* on the spine of one of them. I'm almost sure it did.'

'Well, it probably doesn't matter,' Kevin said airily. He ran a finger round the inside of his collar. 'What did the letter say anyway?'

'Of course it matters!' Alison cried. 'If Logios is real, then part of what Sep said might be true. What if he's been mucking about trying to disprove this theorem 39, and ended up blowing all the power for miles around? It would explain everything!' She blinked. 'What did you just say?'

'What did the letter say? The one marked Urgent?'

'Oh no!' Alison looked at him aghast. 'I put it down on the floor when I started talking to Sep, and then I forgot about it.'

'So it's still up in his room? And you still don't know what it says?'

She shook her head.

'Probably wasn't important,' he said in the voice of someone trying to convince himself. 'That happens all the time. You think a letter's going to be really interesting, then it turns out to be your gran wondering why you haven't thanked her for what she gave you the Christmas before last. Or one of those things from the town hall saying you owe the leisure department £7.59 and they're going to confiscate your library pass. Or someone offering you a timeshare in Majorca. Or—'

'I don't care!' Alison jumped to her feet. 'I know it's probably really boring and not important, but I want to know what's in that letter!'

'Oh good!' Kevin said. 'I'll come too, shall I? Just in case.'

'Just in case what?' Alison asked as they collided in the doorway.

'In case it gives me the creeps sitting down here in the dark waiting for you.'

'Fair enough,' said Alison.

Chapter Three

The letter was gone. Worse, so was the lodger.

Alison stared round the room, head whirling.

The pile of books she had sat on fifteen minutes before was just as she'd left it. So was the table, awash with books, maps, and odds and ends of every description. The candle was still alight, its flame dancing in the draught from the window.

'He can't have gone!' she said in disbelief. 'We'd have heard him. The stairs creak, and the front door jams in wet weather. You've practically got to kick it open. He must be here somewhere.'

'Definitely.' Kevin nodded. He looked round the attic with narrowed eyes. 'Under the bed?'

'Don't be ridiculous!' Alison snapped. 'Why would he hide there?'

'If he was frightened.'

She snorted. 'Up here? Frightened of what?'

Kevin studied his fingernails in a non-committal way. 'Something.'

Muttering, Alison looked under the bed. She found the rest of Sep's book collection, a pair of rusty ice-skates, and a mummified cheese sandwich. There was no sign of the missing lodger.

The only other place big enough to conceal a body – or person, as Alison unreasonably preferred to call it – was the wooden cupboard built into the sloping roof. It was latched on the outside, but as Kevin pointed out, it could have a two-way catch inside the door.

The latch was jammed so tight it wouldn't budge until Alison bashed it with the blade of the ice-skates. Then it broke off entirely, and the door flew open, shooting an avalanche of papers on to their feet.

'My goodness,' Alison said, as the wind caught the sheets of paper and sent them whirling across the room.

'I don't think he's in there,' Kevin said thoughtfully as the sheets of paper settled. He scooped up an armful of papers and tried to stuff them back in the cupboard. This well-meaning attempt triggered a second avalanche that buried him up to the ankles.

'Leave it.' Alison collapsed on the edge of the bed. 'Even if we could get them all back in, we'd never get the door shut. Pile them under the bed with the rest of his junk. I don't expect they're anything interesting, knowing Sep. What's that one?'

Kevin carried the page over to the candle. 'Looks like the start of an essay. Listen: "Compare and contrast the influence of (a) wind speed, (b) humidity and (c) proximity to the ocean upon relocational enchantments, with particular reference to Logios 15, Logios 211 and Logios 536." ' His voice died away as he took in what he'd just said. 'Could be some sort of code.' He looked at her hopefully. 'What have you got?'

Picking up a sheet at random, Alison recited in an expressionless voice: 'Seven modes of invisibility and how to reverse them.' She dropped the sheet and picked up another. 'The theory and practice of spells of binding and unbinding.' She looked at the back of the sheet. 'He got B − + − (?) for it.' She dropped that page too. 'I don't think it's a code, Kevin. I wish Mum was home.'

It was seven forty-five. That meant her mother must have missed the six-thirty fast train. The next one was due at eight-fifteen. Alison mentally added time for getting the car and driving home. 'She'll be here by eight-thirty. You can stay till then, if you like. If your parents won't worry,' she added reluctantly.

To her relief, Kevin said his parents never worried. He went on to explain that he was the youngest in his family. His brother Darren was spending his gap year bicycling across Australia. His sister Becky was teaching English in Bangkok, his other sister Tess was backpacking in Ecuador, and his oldest brother Mike was taking a break from his studies by working on an oil rig.

'I see.' Alison blinked. 'What are you planning to do? When you leave school, I mean.'

He reddened slightly. 'I want to be an accountant. Mum and Dad don't understand it. I keep finding application forms for Operation Raleigh or survival courses in the Cairngorms tucked under my pillow. So they don't mind a bit when I'm late home now and then – it sort of softens the blow.' Without any change of tone he went on, 'Did this Sep person happen to mention whether or not he had a magic carpet?'

Alison looked at him.

He looked back, unabashed. 'He's gone, hasn't he? And the window's open. And that's the sort of thing wizards do.'

'In books,' she said coldly. 'What were you going

29

to suggest we do next? Conjure up the powers of darkness and ask them where he's got to? Look in our crystal ball? This is real life, Kevin. Have a bit of sense!'

'I think we should look around,' he said, not noticeably cast down, 'and see what turns up. Unless you think he'll mind?'

Alison tried to imagine Sep minding anything, and failed. She told Kevin that even if the lodger did mind, it wouldn't matter much. Madman or wizard, he couldn't say boo to a goose.

She added a final scathing comment as she headed for the table by the window. 'Flying carpets! Good grief! If you'd ever met Sep you'd know how ridiculous that was.'

In the darkness, Septimus Similon crouched on all fours in the middle of a small rectangle of foam-backed 100% nylon tufted carpet, and prayed.

Flying was supposed to be one of those skills you never forgot. Like riding a bike, some long-ago instructor had told him. Only he'd never got the hang of a bicycle either.

The darkness tilted and whirled, producing the familar churning in the pit of his stomach. Trying to ignore it, he wrestled with the problem of why the carpet wasn't landing. His last trip to Fentwick's bedsit in Wimbledon had taken no more than ten minutes, but tonight he seemed to have been flying for ever.

Why was his supervisor suddenly so keen to see him anyway? They hadn't had much to say to each other even before Sep had submitted a draft outline of his scheme for refuting Logios. And after . . .

'You can't expect a frogging grant for this!' Fentwick had said woundingly. 'And if you think I'm going to sign your application, think again. Fentwick of Wimbledon is a name that means something. I have my reputation to consider. Drop me a line when you've come up with a serious plan of study. You know the way out. And don't come back till you're summoned,' he had shouted as the crestfallen Sep departed.

So why had Fentwick changed his tune? All Sep could think was that it must have something to do with the detailed outline he had sent Strepticon, Treasurer of the Wizards' Council, to support his claim for a full research grant. Something in it must have made Strepticon sit up and take notice. Then he must have called Fentwick, and Fentwick must have . . .

The journey really was taking an extraordinary length of time. Taking great care not to upset the carpet's balance, Sep lifted one hand and felt cautiously for his pocket compass. It was not unusual to make a mistake in programming a carpet's flight path. Better check it was still travelling due east.

He pressed the compass's back-light button and lifted it closer to his face.

The carpet bucked as he gave a wild start. According to the compass, he was travelling north by northwest!

No, northwest! No – before Sep's baffled eyes the red arrow swung round until it was pointing due west. Southwest . . . south . . .

Sep sunk his head on to the carpet and groaned.

He was travelling in a circle.

'We bissed hib,' the bald man said bitterly. He was veering towards the theory that what he had wasn't a cold but a bad case of flu, or possibly pneumonia. In either case, the last thing he needed was an evening lurking in a damp rhododendron bush waiting for the suspect to return. He blew his nose like a sad foghorn, and went on with sudden clarity, 'We shouldn't have waited. What's a couple of witnesses? They were no one important.'

His companion turned up his collar. 'This time, we go by the rule book. He'll be back sooner or later. Then we wait till everyone's asleep, go in over the roof, and hey presto! Back in Theromantia by morning, as tidy as tadpoles.'

'As frogging wet as tadpoles too,' growled the bald man.

'Shh!' whispered the second agent with sudden urgency. 'Someone's coming.' He whipped out what looked like a calculator from his raincoat pocket and punched three buttons. He looked up, his eyes glittering with triumph. 'And that someone's a wizard.'

'It's him!' the bald man gloated. 'Oldest trick in the book, too; coming back on foot when he left by carpet. Must think we were born yesterday. What we going to use? The old freeze-him-and-bind-him?'

'Say what you like.' The other agent flexed his fingers. 'It does the business. There's no prizes in this game for originality. On the count of three, now.' He held his hand up, listening intently. 'One. Two. Thr—'

And there were absolutely no witnesses.

The assortment of objects on Sep's table might, as Alison said sourly, possibly have appealed to a junk-shop, but it was hard to see what even Sherlock Holmes could have deduced from them.

'Yes? Great,' Kevin said absently. He was supposed to be investigating the debris that had accumulated in and around Sep's bed, but he'd found a treatise called *How to Faffinate Wymmen* and showed every sign of settling down for a good read.

Alison turned back to the table and picked up the map.

This was the kind sold by half the newsagents in Axborough, showing streets and local landmarks like the schools and churches. The common was easy to spot. So was Field End Road. Number thirty-eight, Alison calculated for her own amusement, should be more or less—

She stopped, with her finger poised.

At that exact point there was a tiny hole in the map. As if – yes! She drew in her breath. As if someone had inserted the point of a pair of compasses just there, with a view to drawing a circle.

When she moved the candle closer, she could see the circle itself. It sliced through the common, cutting off the dual carriageway and the underpass. It cut across Webber Street, Park Road, Kingsley Avenue . . .

'Spooky,' Kevin said when summoned to have a look. He caught her eye. 'I mean, it's interesting and a bit scary, but absolutely nothing to worry about. Probably. I was in Webber Street myself this evening, come to think of it. And up on the common. Nothing to worry about at all.' Something told him it wasn't the moment to mention the goat. He didn't want her to think he was seeing things.

Come to that, he didn't want to think that himself.

'And it was all quite normal?'

'Nothing to worry about,' Kevin said for the third time. He almost believed it too.

'Similon, you prize pillock,' thundered a voice from the street. 'Your anteater's just tried to take a chunk out of my ankle. Open up! I want to talk to you!' The house rocked as their visitor tried to kick down the door. 'And when I've talked to you, I want to feed you into a meat grinder and pour you down the nearest drain. Hurry up and *open this door*!'

Armed with the bicycle lamp, Alison peered over the chain at their visitor. 'Sep's not here, I'm afraid. Who shall I say called?'

'Me, of course!' From the crown of his battered cap to the heels of his mud-caked boots, the visitor radiated irritation. 'While you're at it, tell him to call off the anteaters. It's no good hiding. I'll find him sooner or later, and when I do . . .' The threat was left dangling, but Alison gathered that he was seriously displeased.

She jumped as Kevin popped his head over her shoulder. 'He's not hiding. He's vanished. I don't suppose you happen to know if he had a magic carp—'

Mortified, Alison kicked him. 'What he means is . . .' She stopped. Basically, it was impossible to come up with a plausible and at the same time remotely sane explanation of what Kevin had said.

This didn't seem to trouble the stranger. His eyebrows snapped together. 'Vanished? Typical! Well, he can't have gone far, that's certain. Even on a magic carpet . . . But he may have tried.' He looked at Kevin, and a glimmer of approval stirred on the well-wooded slopes of his face. 'Yes, young man, he certainly may have tried. You had best let me in. I am Abernethy Fentwick, Professor Emeritus in Advanced Wizardry, unofficially attached to the University of Mid Middlesex, and if I cannot locate that young idiot, nobody can.'

'Wait a moment.' Alison slammed the door.

'What if he isn't who he makes out?' she muttered fiercely at Kevin. (She had to turn a deaf ear to the inner voice that added, *and what if he is*?) 'He's not coming in without some proof.' And there, despite all Kevin's objections, she stuck.

There are all sorts of ways, as she pointed out, a man can prove who he is. Unfortunately Abernethy Fentwick, if that was who he really was, did not carry a business card, had no letter addressed to himself, and dismissed the suggestion that he might possess a driving licence with a snort of contempt.

Kevin's brainwave didn't go down well either.

'Cast a spell?' Fentwick asked in outrage. 'What do you take me for? Allow me to inform you that I am a wizard, not, as you seem to believe, a performing seal. Wizards do not do tricks.'

Pressed to say what he did do, the professor drew himself up very straight and said stiffly, 'We investigate the essence of things. We find things out. We understand them. That is all you need to know.'

'Are you telling me that's what Sep does too?' Alison demanded, putting her finger on the flaw in this explanation.

Fentwick's eyes flashed. 'Septimus Similon couldn't investigate his way out of a wet paper bag. That is what makes it all the more absurd – criminally irresponsible – and horrifically dangerous – for him to start newting about with Logios 39. What are you doing now?'

She finished unhooking the chain. 'You should have said it was you who rang earlier. It would have saved a lot of trouble. Come in. And as for you,' she said with unnatural calmness to the creature that was trying in vain to lumber up the front step, 'I don't know what you are or where you came from, but you are *not* coming in. Shoo!'

With that she slammed the door.

Chapter Four

Not a glimmer of light rose from the world beneath him. Similon gripped a front corner of the carpet in each shaking hand and pressed gently down. The carpet plummeted earthwards, leaving his stomach somewhere in the clouds.

In the circumstances it was sheer luck that it landed on Westleigh High playing-fields rather than on a roof, or the school railings. The impact catapulted Similon into a sea of mud, but he picked himself up with nothing worse than shock and a grazed cheek from falling on his compass. For the first moment, he stayed crouched on the ground, his ears filled with a roaring noise like the sea. Then he pulled himself together and limped back to the carpet.

Remount, he told himself sternly, trying to sound like Bloxifil, legendary instructor on Aeronautics Part One. Go on, you fool, issue fresh instructions. Show it who's boss. What are you – a wizard or a mouse?

It was no good, he wasn't fooling anyone, least of all himself. The carpet, floating gently in a puddle, knew quite well who was boss as things stood. And what good would it do to remount, when he had no earthly clue what was wrong with the blasted thing? A carpet only flew in a circle if you gave it impossible instructions – and what was impossible about asking it to fly to Wimbledon?

He seated himself gingerly on one corner. The roaring in his head made it difficult to think clearly. Exasperated, he hit himself smartly on the left ear. This hurt, but did nothing to silence the roar. Could he have concussion?

A gust of wind flung rain in his face. The drops trickled down his grazed cheek, stinging like salt.

Salt?

He licked his lips experimentally and frowned.

The rain *was* salty. And mixed with the salt on his lips were other grains that felt like sand.

'Anyone would think I was by the sea,' he

remarked wearily. And then: 'The sea? Oh no!'

You cannot choose the moment when inspiration is going to visit you. You can be under an apple-tree, in the bath, watching television, trying to remember where you put your science homework – it makes no difference. When the truth dawns, it dawns, whether you want it to or not.

Thus it came to pass that Similon, sitting on a wet carpet in the middle of a muddy football field, understood at last why his carpet had flown in a circle.

Feeling extremely sorry – largely for himself – he buried his face in his hands and groaned.

Abernethy Fentwick swept up the stairs like a whirlwind, sprang through Sep's doorway, and immediately trod on a large cat that was squatting menacingly on a pillowcase just inside the door.

While Kevin helped him up, the cat vanished, growling, under the bed. Alison lifted the hem of the bedspread and peered into the shadows. 'Sorry. I don't know what it's doing here. Mum would have a fit if she knew. It must have come in through the window.'

'You shut the window when we were up here before.' Kevin spoke cheerfully. Luckily Alison didn't know him well enough to realise that this meant he was seriously alarmed. 'Don't you remember?'

Alison did remember. The cat's green eyes squinted at her out of the gloom. Its tail flicked from side to side, raising a small dust-storm from the carpet, and a throaty rumble sounded deep in its chest. It looked to her like the sort of cat you didn't touch without gardening gloves.

Letting the bedspread drop, she stood up. 'It's not doing any harm there. Sep can sort it out when he comes back.'

'If he comes back.' Fentwick limped across to the desk and sat down heavily. 'Which will be a miracle. What a night to take out a carpet! Low cloud, poor visibility, high winds, and on top of all that, Logios 39 up the spout!' He gave a snort, then added, 'We all know what that means.'

'No, we don't!' Alison cried. 'Who is this Logios everyone's going on about? And what's so special about Logios 39?'

Abernethy Fentwick raised his bushy brows. 'Dear me. What primitive parts I currently inhabit. Lazarus Logios, you shocking ignoramus, was none other than the greatest theoretical wizard of all time. The seven hundred and seventy-seven theorems of which he is the author constitute the main body of knowledge in every corner of the galaxy where these things are the subject of serious study. I strongly suggest you purchase the handy 79-volume pocket edition of his works from any good bookshop.'

'Nonsense,' Alison said crossly. 'You're making this up. I've never seen his books anywhere.'

'The nearest good bookshop,' he continued serenely, 'is on the lower level of 25 Castle Walk, in the town of Stolk, capital of Theromantia. It is a mere two dimensions distant when the wind is from the east, and I could take you there myself this instant if it weren't for the problems that nincompoop Similon has brought down upon us. Not to mention it being strictly against the Wizard's Code,' he added as an obvious afterthought.

'What about Logios 39?' Kevin asked, rather pale.

'Logios 39 deals with spells of enclosing.' Fentwick spoke with heavy patience. 'Here—' He scooped up a book from the floor. 'Read it yourself. It begins on page 519, if my memory serves.'

Buckling slightly at the knees, Kevin laid the book on top of the mess on Sep's table. Neither he nor Alison was much surprised when it opened automatically at page 519. Halfway down the right-hand page, a bold heading stood out in a sea of tiny, cramped script.

Theorem 39

Ye ſpelleſ of encloſinge be neceſſarily ſmall in ſcope and tranſient. Yere maxſimum dymenſioune be as followeſ . . .

'Enclofing?' Alison asked, skipping the rest of the paragraph. 'That means "enclosing", right? So what he's saying is that—'

'Spells of enclosing are necessarily small in scope and transient,' Fentwick finished. 'Theromantic enclosures – magical enclosures as you laymen call them – are inherently unstable. The larger they are, the greater the instability. Logios demonstrates that with the utmost elegance over the next twenty-five pages. It's the closest thing to a perfect theorem the world is ever likely to see.' The wizard sighed. 'Unfortunately it seems to have one minor drawback. As that blithering idiot Similon has taken it upon himself to demonstrate, it isn't true.'

Alison looked at him blankly while her brain went into overdrive.

Question: How can a person demonstrate that a theromantic enclosure is not necessarily small in scope and transient?

Answer: By creating one that isn't. The circle on the map flashed before her eyes, complete with the tiny pin-prick at its centre on Field End Road.

'What's the opposite of "transient"?' she asked aloud.

Kevin looked hopefully at Fentwick. 'Not very transient?'

Oblivious to the two pairs of eyes willing him to nod, the wizard shook his head. 'The opposite of transient is *not* transient,' he said in a sombre voice. 'Unless I'm wrong – and that hasn't happened since 1954 – Septimus Similon has managed to cast a spell enclosing a substantial area of land within a barrier that is impenetrable, immovable and permanent.'

'And we're inside!' As the truth hit her, Alison turned to Kevin in horror. 'That's what the circle means! He's enclosed this whole part of Axborough. We're trapped! We can't get out, and no one outside can get in. Ever!'

Kevin swallowed. If she was right, it was going to be on balance a good thing that his parents never worried.

'Our only hope,' Fentwick continued grimly, 'is to locate the creator of the enclosure, and get him to try to put it into reverse. Before it's too late. Every second counts.'

'He had a letter,' Alison said. 'He didn't open it when I brought it up, and when I came back with Kevin, it was gone, and so was he. Oh, if only we knew what it said or had a clue which way he went! For heaven's sake, Kevin, stop that!'

Ever since Fentwick had mentioned the need to locate Similon, Kevin had been shifting from one foot to the other, opening his mouth to speak, and then pretending he had to cough instead. Under Alison's scowl he said sheepishly, 'Don't suppose this would help, by any chance?' He brought one hand out from behind his back. Nestling in it was something that looked like a battered croquet ball, held together with bits of sticking-plaster. Avoiding Alison's eye he went on rapidly, 'I don't suppose it's anything important, but I found it under the pillow, and I thought, I mean to say, I sort of wondered whether it might just possibly be a . . . well, the fact is,' he decided to come clean, 'I thought it might be a crystal ball.'

'*That*?' Alison said, incredulous. 'That's not crystal, for crying out loud.'

'It certainly isn't,' Fentwick agreed, stretching out his hand. He flicked a fingernail against the ball's surface, which gave out a strange, high-pitched *ping*. 'It's not even chryomantine, which makes a decent second-best. What we have here, Logios help us, is a ball botched up in some back street of Stolk out of recycled querulite.'

'I didn't really think it was crystal,' said Kevin, blushing harder than ever. 'I'll put it back, shall I?'

The wizard's brows snapped down. 'Put it back? Don't be ridiculous. Even querulite is better than nothing. Stop dithering and let me have it. Come on, come on!'

Querulite balls are chronically cloudy and prone to snowstorms of interference. Squinting into it briefly made Alison's eyes water and her head throb. More to the point, it didn't work.

'What makes you think that?' Fentwick asked in a superior voice.

Alison very nearly stamped her foot. How could it be working, she demanded, when what it showed was impossible? Either Fentwick had set it up wrong, or the whole thing was broken. Whichever way you looked at it, it was a waste of time expecting it to furnish new information.

'Don't look, if it upsets you.' Fentwick went on gazing intently into the ball, rotating it gently in the palms of both hands. 'But I assure you, it is far from broken. I'll begin by looking north. Hmm. Maximum range appears to be one Theromantic mile – the radius of the circle, I imagine. Here goes.'

One mile north of 38 Field End Road was halfway up Webber Street. Where, according to the ball, pine trees sprouted from the tarmac. The goat Kevin had met on his bicycle still stood by the chasm, looking slantways out of the ball with yellow eyes.

'It hasn't moved,' Kevin exclaimed, taken by surprise. 'It was there hours ago.'

'Ridiculous!' Alison said, unable to turn away. 'If you saw it, why didn't you say?'

'Obviously because you wouldn't have believed him,' Fentwick commented. 'Interesting. No sign of Similon, however. Better try elsewhere.'

One mile due east of the attic, boulders blocked the A519. Above the boulders, a rocky slope led up to a dilapidated castle, draped with ivy.

'That's a nice touch,' Fentwick murmured, pointing appreciatively. 'Look how perfectly the two wings of that ruined arch meet. Looks easy, but it isn't. Bit of an artist in his own way, Similon. We've underestimated him, I think. Don't know when I've seen a better illusion. The spitting image of Stolk Castle too.'

'Illusion?' Alison tore her eyes away from the ball. 'You mean it's . . .'

Fentwick smiled with sweet insincerity. 'Dear me, you didn't think it was real, did you?'

She gaped at him.

'Look!' Fentwick crowed. 'He's even put a wolf with bloodstained fangs on top of that crag to the right. Priceless! I'll use the zoom, then you can see it properly.'

'Don't bother,' Alison said coldly. She looked at Kevin. 'I suppose you guessed they were illusions all along.' She was torn between irritation and relief. It wasn't that she was fond of Webber Street, or the A519. As bits of scenery went, they left her cold. But they were more than bits of scenery; they were part of her life. She'd fallen over in Webber Street when she was four, and had to have three stitches – she could still feel the scar on her knee. Her mother

drove home from the station every night along the A519. Where was she tonight, Alison wondered, blinking furiously. Moving heaven and earth to cross a permanent, immovable barrier to reach home, and her daughter?

It was definitely not the moment to think about that. Alison sniffed fiercely and said, in an almost normal voice, 'What are you waiting for? If Sep's not there, you'll have to look somewhere else.'

One mile due south, waves lashed the wall of Westleigh High's new science block, and a large porcupine waddled across a sandy waste that had once been the junior netball courts. The porcupine, as Kevin said, looked very convincing. So did the winged, two-headed beast patrolling the moonlit sky a mile due west, above the common.

'Aha! Thelamungus . . .' Fentwick stared raptly into Similon's ball for a full minute before condescending to explain that Logios had defeated the thelamungus in a legendary battle above the streets of Stolk some two hundred years previously. Similon had probably added it to the illusions guarding his enclosure as what Fentwick called a *jeu d'esprit*, a flourish to impress his fellow wizards.

The thelamungus swooped down and plucked something from the grass at the edge of the pond. It shook its heads playfully. One curved beak opened, and a limp shape like a glove flew across the road, hit a lamp-post, and fell messily on the pavement. 'It's very good,' the professor said with reluctant admiration. 'I've no idea how he managed that. It's quite extraordinary.'

'It's horrible.' Alison's voice shook. 'Can't you move on? We're no nearer finding Sep than when we started.' She gave Kevin the best smile she could. He was looking a bit green round the gills, and she liked him the better for it. 'At least it isn't real – that's one comfort.'

'It isn't?' said Kevin with a start. 'I mean, it isn't.'

The thelamungus spat out a mouthful of fur and bones and settled down to preen its feathers. Kevin's gaze took in the bloody claws, the dripping beak, and the small, sad stain on the pavement. 'He must be awfully clever, your Sep.' He gave his brightest smile. It was at moments like this that he felt particularly glad he was going to be an accountant. Accountants never had to cope with scenes like the one he was witnessing. He averted his eyes hurriedly. 'Lucky for us it's not real, eh?'

Fentwick nodded. 'Lucky for everyone.'

Chapter Five

When Alison's alarm-clock went off at seven-fifteen, it came as a relief: she'd been having a terrible dream. Sep came into it, and so did a boy from school whose name she couldn't remember. Darrell? Gavin? Burrowing into her pillow, she flung out an arm and groped for the off-switch.

It wasn't there.

Nor was the clock.

Nor was the stereo it should have been sitting on.

Bolt upright, eyes wide, she peered at her bedside table in disbelief. The clock was there after all, but it was in the wrong place; well below mattress-level, resting crookedly on top of a wooden recorder and a mouth-organ.

'Spooky,' said a voice from the floor.

A familiar face peered up at her out of a lumpy brown sleeping bag. Kevin! she thought with surprise – that's who the boy in the dream was. Only he didn't seem to be a dream after all. And if he was real, what about the rest?

'Fentwick!' she exclaimed, remembering. He'd chivvied them out of the attic at midnight, on the grounds that he had to spend the night thinking. Maybe he'd found a solution? Or found Sep? 'Come on, Kevin!' She bundled the quilt round her shoulders, wriggled her feet into her slippers and headed for the door.

Kevin didn't budge. 'I'm not dressed,' he objected, sleeping bag clutched to his chin. 'Where's the bathroom?'

'What? Oh, along there.' As she bounded towards the stairs, she flapped a hand vaguely. 'Just look and you'll find it.'

Her hopes fizzled out as soon as she opened the attic door. Sep's bed was empty, except for the cat asleep on his pillow. The professor was snoring gently at Sep's table, his head pillowed on an open book. Judging by the sea of crumpled papers on the floor at his feet, solutions had been hard to come by.

She stepped forward, and cleared her throat. 'Ahem. *Ahem!*'

Fentwick lifted his head groggily. 'Similon?' He blinked at her. 'Oh! It's you. Almost nodded off. He's not back, I take it?'

She shook her head. 'Have you thought of anything?'

He sat up straight and glared. The edge of the book had left a red ridge running north to south down his right cheek – Alison tried not to stare at it. 'Of course I've thought of something. That's what wizards are for, thinking. I've thought of everything from a formula for gravitational reversement to a new way to classify newts. Unfortunately, so far, none of it helps. Go and get dressed. You'll be late for school.'

Force of habit took her downstairs, but on the first-floor landing, outrage set in. 'I can't believe this,' she growled at Kevin, coming up from the hall below. 'He wants us to go to school! Here we are, cut off from everywhere, probably for ever, and he expects us to carry on as if nothing's happened!' She blinked as he reached the top of the stairs. The bathroom lay the other way. 'Where've you been?'

He looked embarrassed. 'You know. I told you.' He saw her expression. 'What's the matter? I locked the back door again when I came in.'

As she dived past him, she thought how nice it

would be to think he'd made a huge, Kevin-style mistake, but something told her that, today, life wasn't so simple. Sure enough, moments later she found herself staring at the small outhouse that had sprung up in the back garden. Its function was depressingly clear.

Kevin had not made a mistake.

'I wasn't sure what to do with the spade,' he confessed, hovering at her shoulder. 'I was about to ask.'

'Don't.' She shut the door with a bang. 'I've never seen it before in my life. And what on earth is *that*?'

The rustic brick structure in the middle of the rockery turned out on inspection to be a crude well. Kevin cranked a bucket up from the depths and said it worked, sort-of.

The open hearth in the kitchen probably worked too, if they'd had any firewood to fill it, or a ton of steel wool to scour the huge, battered cooking-pot that squatted on the shelf where the saucepans used to be.

Kevin – who had fifteen years' experience of looking on the bright side – said, 'Mmm . . . interesting.' He lifted the lid of a metal bin in one corner, gasped, and slammed it down again. 'Rats too! It's really . . . different.' He moved to the far end of the kitchen, humming under his breath.

'Hmm! I detect a strong flavour of Theromantia,'

was Fentwick's verdict when dragged downstairs. 'Don't keep asking why. I don't know why. Logios has nothing to say about sealed systems like this, for the simple reason that they're meant to be impossible.'

He lifted the lid of the bin, and raised an eyebrow. 'You've got rats.'

'We never used to,' Alison said defensively.

'You have now. And I don't wish to appear critical, but there's a dead bird under the table. Someone should clear it up.'

The person in question was plainly not going to be the speaker, who stationed himself at the window and frowned out at the garden with the air of someone who is making a major contribution to the sum of human knowledge. Equally plainly, it was not going to be Kevin who, after one glance under the table, sneezed and claimed to be allergic to feathers. Muttering darkly, Alison found a dustpan and brush. How did a huge pigeon get inside anyway, she wondered, as she tipped the contents of the dustpan on to the compost heap. Nothing made sense.

'I'm not so sure,' Fentwick said seriously when she came back in. 'Think about it. When Similon cut us off from the rest of the world yesterday, he left all kinds of loose ends dangling – electricity lines, water pipes, drains, that sort of thing—'

'Trust Sep not to worry about details like that,' said Alison, through gritted teeth.

'Fair's fair,' Fentwick said, rising to the defence of a colleague. 'The man's a wizard, not a plumber. Now suppose, just suppose, his system won't tolerate loose ends and inconsistencies, what then?'

Alison and Kevin looked at each other blankly. What indeed?

'I'll tell you what.' Fentwick's eyes sparkled. It struck Alison that in a peculiar sort of way he was enjoying himself. 'Reality has to reshape itself, that's what. It has to knit up the loose ends the best way it can! No electricity, so no electric cooker. An open hearth instead. No water supply, so no running water. And so on.'

'No telephone wires,' she exclaimed, suddenly inspired. 'That's how the bird got here. It must have been a carrier-pigeon!'

Kevin gazed at her, struck dumb with admiration.

'Well, obviously.' Fentwick tried to convey the impression that he'd made that connection hours ago. 'If you ask me, what we are witnessing here is reality regrowth. Which means, in case you need to have it spelled out, that reality is regrowing over the damage Similon inflicted on it, the way the body grows new skin over a wound.'

Kevin opened his mouth, and then shut it again without saying anything. She knew what had been

56

on the tip of his tongue, though, and for once she agreed.

The idea of reality regrowth was distinctly spooky.

What if you didn't want a new reality, she asked herself as she pulled on her jeans. What if you were one of those boring people who liked stereos and non-stick saucepans, who wanted a telephone, not a carrier-pigeon? What if you enjoyed watching *Neighbours* on TV when you came home from school? What if, in a funny sort of way, you missed your mother? There had to be a way to put things right.

'School,' said Fentwick positively, 'that's the place to look for answers. You can't stay home every time things go a little bit wrong. All right,' he conceded, 'a big bit wrong. The point is, education matters. This isn't the end of the world, you know.'

'It isn't?'

Irony is wasted on wizards. 'Certainly not. It's more like the beginning. Go to school.' He swept them towards the door. 'Who knows? – you might learn something new. In fact,' his eyebrows shot up as a thought struck him, 'I should think it's highly probable you will.'

Alison was still inclined to mutiny. 'And where will you be?'

'Here. Someone has to man the centre of the circle.

And that idiot is bound to come back sooner or later. After all, where else can he go?'

Cold more biting than any he had ever felt before roused Similon.

Hours of despairing thought had yielded exactly one idea. When he drew the circle on the map the day before, he had put the pencil point down somewhere at the beginning, and lifted it off again at the end. If the barrier had any weak spot at all, it seemed to him that it must lie at one of those points, where the spell and the circle began or ended.

So far so good. If he could remember where his pencil first touched the map, he'd be halfway there. But of course, he couldn't.

He rolled the damp carpet up and tucked it beneath his arm. All he could do was make his way round the barrier, testing it as he went. If there was a weak spot, he'd find it, and then . . .

He huddled deeper into his overcoat. He didn't know what he would do then, but he was going to have to do *something*.

He braced himself and turned to face the gale that blew from the sea.

The walk to school was a sobering experience.

There wasn't a car or bus to be seen, at a time when the streets should have been seething with traffic. The rooftops looked stark, stripped bare of television aerials and satellite dishes. Every other gatepost they passed seemed to have a horse tethered to it. A herd of cows was grazing the grass verge outside the milk depot, and bales of hay and water troughs were lined up at the petrol station. Worse still were the expressions on the faces of the people they met – suspicious, frightened, angry, or baffled. At the junction of Field End Road and Trent Avenue, a woman ran out, clutching a baby, to ask for advice as they crossed the road.

What advice could they possibly give?

'You've got no water? And there's a horse in your garage?' Alison heard herself repeating helplessly. 'I'm sorry, I don't know who you ought to complain to.' She shot a glance at Kevin. 'I don't think there *is* anyone.'

'You could let the horse out,' he suggested thoughtfully. 'And give it some food too – is there a metal bin in your kitchen? Well, look inside and you'll find oats or something like that. Horses like those. Oh, and if you need water, there ought to be a well in the back garden. Try the rockery. No, it's no trouble.' He waved away an attempt at thanks. 'Glad to be able to help.'

'I don't think you ought to talk like that,' Alison muttered forcefully as the woman retreated up her front path, casting dubious glances over her shoulder as she went. 'I know you were only trying to help. I know she was upset. Everyone's upset, including me, Kevin. And I'm going to be a whole lot more upset if you go giving people the idea that we know more than they do about all this. You know what's going to happen next? They'll think we did it.'

Kevin's face creased into the expression of deep thought it occasionally wore in chemistry lessons when he was wondering where he'd put his Travelcard. 'I see what you mean. Sorry. Won't happen again.'

'It had better not.'

'We don't know much more than them, after all, do we?'

'Try and get it into your head; we don't know *anything*.'

'There won't be anyone at school to ask questions anyway,' he observed soothingly, elaborating, 'well, you'd have to be crazy to keep a school open on a day like this.'

Which just went to show, she reflected, how little he knew Mr Dempsey. Some headmasters might use the end of life on Earth as most people knew it as an excuse to send pupils home, but not him.

'Alison Braythwayte, Kevin Young, you're late,' Mr Dempsey rapped out as he spotted them lurking in the doorway. 'Don't stand gawping. Sit down and listen. As you would be aware if you had arrived at the proper hour, an emergency timetable will apply until further notice. Get your rough books out and take notes. Here is the roster for sandbag duty.'

As they headed for the kitchens at midday along with a handful of shell-shocked students, Alison was conscious of a grudging respect for the headmaster. Faced with a situation no head teacher had ever had to tackle before, he was coming through with flying colours.

'Right!' Mr Dempsey stationed himself in the centre of the kitchen, and squared his shoulders. 'Samantha, Jeremy, Parvind: you're on firewood patrol. Try the hedge outside my study. Roshan and Miriam, find steel wool and scour the cauldron. Yes, of course you take out the dead bat first – and the frog, and whatever else you find there. Kindly use your common sense.' With Kevin and Alison tagging obediently behind, he swept out in search of provisions.

A minute later all three stood in the storeroom doorway, temporarily speechless.

'Er – what should we take?' Kevin asked at last.

Mr Dempsey seemed at a loss, and Alison could see why.

Gone was the usual storeroom stock; the jumbo-sized vats of baked beans, the catering packs of fish-fingers and processed peas. In their place were shelf upon shelf of glass preserving jars and sinister brown packages. Some were labelled, some weren't. Some didn't need to be.

Even if you've never set eyes on one before, there's something unmistakable about pickled mice.

No wonder Mr Dempsey had lost his voice.

'You know what?' Kevin said, 'I think I'll give lunch a miss. I'm not that hungry.'

Three-quarters of the way through his circuit, Similon was cold, hungry and tired. Somewhere along the way – just after he met the woman who screamed that there was a waterfall in the middle of her kitchen, to be precise – it had sunk in that unless he put things right soon, a lot of people were going to be cross.

He had a hunch that they were going to be cross with him.

He wished he'd thought of that before.

He couldn't think why he hadn't.

All the same, the sight of the jagged skyline above the A519 produced a surge of pride. No two ways about it, the mountains were the finest illusions he had ever achieved. Quite apart from the extraordinary visual effect, the howling of wolves from the slopes was enough to curdle the blood.

He frowned. Strange, but he couldn't remember

weaving that particular illusion. There it was all the same, though, working like – well, like magic. He smiled sadly. From the cries on the wind, you'd have thought there were dozens of wolves, not just six.

If only Fentwick were there to hear it, he thought wistfully. Or Bloxifil, or the others who always sneered at him. If only they could see the barrier just once, and salute his work, before he had to destroy it for ever...

He sighed. No point wishing. Fentwick was in Wimbledon, and Wimbledon might as well be in another galaxy.

As he wearily stood up, a ray of sun fell on the ramparts of the castle far above, and he had to fight down a wave of homesickness. It was so very like the castle he had used as his model, the place where he had spent six happy – or very nearly happy – years as an apprentice. All that was missing was the green and gold flag of Theromantia that flew from the flagpole of Stolk Castle and nowhere else. Similon would have regarded it as the height of disrespect – amounting to sacrilege – to conjure up a replica of the emblem that stood for the power of the Wizards' Council. He had deliberately left his flagpole bare.

This made it something of a puzzle to see a flag fluttering on the battlements above.

He stepped off the road. He knew the barrier would block his path after a few paces, but he couldn't walk on without taking a closer look.

Up in Sep's attic, Fentwick had a crick in his neck from peering into the querulite ball.

The night before, the range of the ball had been one mile. He had no doubt about that, and no trouble understanding it either. From the ball's point of view, the world ended at the barrier. Nothing existed on the other side.

Last night, he had at least known where he was.

Then came morning . . .

The first time he picked up the ball, around nine o'clock, he found that the horizon had shifted outwards quarter of a mile. By noon the range was more like two miles. Now, in mid-afternoon, the castle perched above the A519 was not merely a picturesque shape on the skyline; he could view it in close-up. He could stand on the battlements and gaze out on the panorama of mountains unrolling eastwards, on and on and on. Similon's illusions were spreading outwards like ripples in a pond.

So far, so bad. But it didn't stop there. When it occurred to him to look closer to home, Fentwick received a worse jolt. Three-quarters of a mile from where he sat chewing his fingernails, pine trees had sprouted through the tarmac in Webber Street.

The ripples were spreading inwards too.

Which was impossible.

Swivelling the ball once more, Fentwick spotted something more profoundly shocking than all the rest. Somebody had crossed the invisible boundary between reality and illusion! A long stone's throw from the solid surface of the A519, a tiny figure was roosting precariously in an imaginary tree, halfway up an illusory slope towards a fictitious castle!

The figure looked terribly familiar . . . After a short battle with the zoom, Fentwick found himself staring into a haggard face streaked with dirt and blood. He had no difficulty recognising its owner.

'Snap out of it, man!' the wizard shouted as Similon lost a shoe to an unpleasantly athletic wolf. 'You know as well as I do those animals aren't real! For the love of Logios, you made them! Pull yourself together and get down!'

But there the tiny figure stayed.

In the end, something close to embarrassment made Fentwick change the setting. As he stared blankly at a flickering image of Axborough Common, he shook his head. He considered himself broad-minded, but it made him go hot and cold all over to think of the spectacle he'd just witnessed: a wizard, fourth-class, cowering up a tree, terrified by his own illusions! What had the world come to when a wizard of any class could be so gullible?

Cupping the ball in the palms of his hands, Fentwick made himself focus on it properly. All at once it had his full attention.

He was looking at a bloodstained bundle of feathers. Once – quite recently – it must have been a crow or blackbird, but it was never going to be that or anything else again. With a start, he realised what the question was that had been nagging for his attention.

Where the hell was the thelamungus?

Thud! The cat yowled and vanished under the bed as something landed meatily on the roof.

Alison was on the late afternoon sea-watch when she glanced to her right and saw a figure at the water's edge. She heard Kevin shout something, but the words were lost in the wind as she ran down the beach.

'Sep!' she yelled, dizzy with relief. 'You're just in time! The tide's coming in. Sep?'

She was close enough by then to see that his overcoat was ripped from collar to hem, one sleeve flapped loose, and there were dark stains at the shoulder and cuff. He moved like a sleepwalker, ignoring the waves that lapped at his feet. 'What's happened? Are you all right? Sep, watch out!'

He staggered slightly as a wave soaked him up to the knees, but he righted himself and waded on.

'Strepticon's here,' he said as if that explained everything. 'I saw him up by the castle. The rest must be here too – Catterat, Bloxifil . . .'

'Sep!' Alison shrieked, as another wave swamped him up to his waist. 'Come back, it's dangerous!'

'I've got to find the weak point in the barrier, or I'm—'

The words ended in a gurgle as the waters closed over his head.

Chapter Six

'It's not that I'm ungrateful,' Alison said without much regard for the truth. 'I suppose Mr Dempsey meant well. You probably meant well too, Kevin.'

'Yes, actually I did.' Kevin sounded touchy, which Alison was inclined to put down to his dress. While she had been lucky enough to find a striking black lycra bodysuit, leg-warmers, and a fluffy angora sweater in the girls' lost property box, the boys' lost property had offered thinner pickings. Kevin had emerged wearing a puce tracksuit whose smell alone would have clouded the sunniest temperament. 'I thought you were being swept out to sea. I still think you were being swept out to sea,' he added pugnaciously.

There was no way she was prepared to let him get away with that. 'I do have my bronze life-saving,' she said witheringly. 'I was letting – *letting* – the riptide take us out. When it died down—'

'Where would that have been? Off Newfoundland?'

'— I was going to swim parallel with the shore, until the waves washed us in. Everything was under control. Until you and Mr Dempsey ran me down with that stupid raft, we were in absolutely no danger. Even then, I'd have been all right if you hadn't tried to pull me up and fallen in on top of me.'

'You're heavier than I thought you'd be,' Kevin shouted. 'And I get seasick.'

'Exactly,' she shouted back – for heaven's sake, now he was implying that she weighed too much! 'You get seasick, you can't swim. Don't you agree it would make more sense if you stayed on dry land in future?'

He had begun a confused but spirited reply when a groan from the couch behind them brought about a temporary halt to hostilities.

'It's no good groaning, Sep,' said Alison severely. 'Mr Dempsey and the others won't be long. I've told them all about what you've done. It's up to you to find a way out of this mess. On top of everything else, we're almost cut off.' The view from the staffroom testified that she was right. 'We could be marooned here for days – for ever! You've got to *think*.'

The occupant of the couch groaned again. 'All I can think about is *them*.' He shrunk down inside the cricketing sweater Kevin had filched from lost property on his behalf. 'Catterat and the others. What are they going to do when they find me? Do you think they'll blame me for everything?'

'Yes. You *are* to blame for everything, Sep.' Alison pointed this out, as she later explained to Kevin, purely in the interests of accuracy, but it might have been better left unsaid.

The wizard sat up, trembling with passion. 'But I told you, I didn't mean anything like this to happen. It was a harmless technical exercise.' His voice broke. 'I thought people would be pleased with me. I thought I'd get a Wizard of the Year nomination. How did it go so horribly wrong?'

With a reproachful look at Alison, Kevin reached out to pat the wizard's shoulder. 'It's all right. Nobody's going to blame you. You mustn't worry.'

'Oh, Sep – I'm sorry.' Alison ran her fingers through her damp hair, which stuck up in spikes, giving her the appearance of an exasperated rabbit.

'I know I shouldn't go on about how stupid you were, but I can't help it. Everywhere I look, something reminds me. Oh Sep, how could you, *could* you, ever have done such a crazy, wicked, idiotic thing?'

Sep cowered back on the couch and then rebounded with a cry of anguish.

'Now look what you've done!' Kevin glared at her. 'You just can't stop, can you? Can't you see he's feeling awful? What are you trying to do, make him jump out the window?'

While Alison was still too stunned to speak, Sep squirmed to reach back behind him. 'No, it's not what she said – there's something sharp down here, a spike or a buckle – ha!' He produced the object with a flourish. 'It's someone's bag.'

Alison blinked at the battered navy-blue backpack in disbelief. 'That's not someone's,' she said slowly. 'It's mine.'

She had only lost it yesterday. So why did it feel as if it belonged to another world, another Alison?

She undid the buckle and opened the flap. She felt another pang as she saw the familiar thick green folder inside. What a relief it would have been to see it just twenty-four hours ago.

'My history notes are still here.' She fished the folder out, balanced it on the arm of the couch, and turned to the zipped side pocket. 'My bus pass is gone, though, and so is the money – no, wait!' The pocket was deep and narrow, which meant groping for small objects, but a moment later she withdrew her hand in triumph. 'They must have missed these – oh!'

The coins nestling in her palm were not pennies, as she had taken for granted. They were thin silver discs, larger than a pound coin but much lighter. The side facing her said ONE DUCAT in raised letters. When she turned one over, the other side showed a cloaked figure waving a stick. The lettering there was smaller, but perfectly legible: LONG LIVE THEROMANTIA!

'Aha! Reality regrowth again,' she heard Kevin say – for all the world as if he were greeting an old friend rather than watching their world turn upside down by several more degrees. Sep, with whom she sympathised, sunk his head in his hands with another groan. Kevin burbled on happily, 'I was wondering whether we'd seen the last of all that. Are you sure it hasn't given you a substitute for your bus pass? Do you mind if I—?'

Alison whisked the bag out of his reach. 'You bet I mind! What's in here is mine, and *if* anything is, I'm going to be the one to find it. Go through your own pockets, and let me go through mine.'

Kevin looked without enthusiasm at his anorak,

which was steaming gently on a chair in front of the fire. 'My stuff's wet.'

'That's not my fault – oh!' Alison couldn't help gasping again as her schoolbag yielded its second secret. She laid the rectangle of card on her folder and smoothed the edges down. 'Kevin,' she said in a strange voice, 'stop rummaging in your coat and take a look at this. What on earth does it mean?'

TO WHOM IT MAY CONCERN
The bearer whose likeness appears on the reverse is entitled to commandeer any and all means of transportation from fellow members of the Organisation (discount rates apply Tuesdays and Fridays, from May to August)
DOWN WITH THE WIZARDS!

'It is a sort of pass!' Kevin sounded gratified and mildly startled. 'I wonder what the Organisation is? They don't think much of wizards by the sound of it. Is there a picture of you on the other side?'

Alison looked, gave a squeak of horror, and pressed the card tight against her chest.

'It's not me. It's someone else,' she said, very fast. 'I'm going to tear it up!' Then to her astonishment and that of the others, she burst into tears.

Hunched so low over the querulite ball that his nose bumped its pitted surface, Fentwick was caught off-guard as a firework display erupted smack in front of his eyeballs.

Even as he rubbed furiously at his eyes, his brain was racing. Interference like that indicated a carpet lift-off. Who in Axborough could possibly be using a carpet? As the answer leaped at him, he lunged for the ball with both hands.

Similon!

'Where are you, you fool?' he muttered, wrestling with the viewfinder. 'Catterat himself couldn't fly in these condi—'

He stopped.

He was looking at the landing-square on the castle tower. In the centre of the square, a group of ashen-faced wizards disembarked from a carpet. No citizen of Stolk City would have had any trouble recognising them, and Fentwick had reason to know them well.

The grizzled figure being sick over the edge of the battlements was none other than Catterat, Theromantia's Chief Wizard.

The sorry-looking specimen crawling in a circle was Catterat's right-hand man Bloxifil, oldest member of the Wizards' Council. The others –

Nebukar and Trebox – were no less eminent in theromantic circles.

Why weren't they all back home, passing a motion of censure on Similon, or arguing into the night over the interpretation of a tricky theorem? What were they doing in the wrong dimension, smack in the middle of Similon's illusions?

Something curdled in the pit of Fentwick's stomach.

He groped blindly for the viewfinder. Any castle could have crumbling battlements, a round tower, and all the rest, but only one castle was entitled to fly the official flag of Theromantia. That privilege belonged to Stolk Castle, seat of the Wizards' Council. A quick inspection of the battlements should settle his fears once and for all.

If the flag wasn't there, he could heave a sigh of relief and get back to working out how in the name of Logios they were going to dismantle the barrier. If the flag *was* there . . . At the mere thought, Fentwick – a lifetime non-believer – shuddered and muttered a prayer.

If the flag was there, reality regrowth was too mild a term for what was going on. What could you call it when two incompatible dimensions got mixed up together?

Reality chaos?

Anarchy?

Whatever you called it, what it spelled was disaster.

In his haste to inspect the battlements, Fentwick caught the edge of the viewfinder with a fingernail and sent it spinning. Tiny images cartwheeled before his eyes like pieces of a jigsaw puzzle caught in a whirlwind: Bloxifil's left foot, the edge of the carpet, Nebukar's grey face, the whirling stars. Then, as he fought to regain control, suddenly, unmistakably, there it was – the top of the flagpole.

Crowned with the Theromantian flag.

The building perched above the A519 was not an uncannily skilful replica of Stolk Castle, it was the real thing; the powerhouse of Theromantia itself. Complete with cargo of resident wizards!

Somehow or other – Fentwick's brain refused at that point to contemplate how – in creating his barrier, Similon had managed to splice Axborough on to Theromantia. Inside the permanent, irreversible barrier . . .

It says a lot for the strict methods under which wizards are trained that a second later, when the thelamungus ripped through the roofing felt, even in a state of shock Fentwick had the presence of mind to snatch up the nearest volume of Logios before he ran for his life.

In the staffroom at Westleigh High, the three

occupants were in the process of coming to terms with a cluster of disconcerting discoveries.

Failing to come to terms might be a better description.

'That is not me,' Kevin repeated stubbornly. He had been saying the same ever since unearthing a slender gold card from his soggy anorak pocket. He showed every sign of being prepared to continue in the same vein indefinitely. His ears had gone red, a sign he was upset.

Alison, on the other hand, had revived with miraculous speed. 'It looks like you,' she said combatively. If being ready to argue the toss from morning to night was any indication, she was now fully recovered from whatever had thrown her earlier on.

'It does *not* look like me.' He lunged forward and succeeded in recapturing the card. 'I don't wear tights!'

'It's got your name on it.'

'It has not! My name is not Kevin Son of Grork.'

Alison gave this short shrift. 'It's Kevin, though. And I think the picture looks like you, in a funny way.' She appealed over her shoulder. 'Doesn't it, Sep?'

'Yes. I mean, no. Who cares?' Similon, who had his own problems, continued to leaf furiously through the sheets he had extracted from her history folder, uttering whinnies of indignation. 'This is disgraceful! It simply is not true! Logios was *not* a minor wizard whose theories were refuted by Baxtenbrat in the second century. It's absolute nonsense.' He regarded Alison with unusual sternness. 'Are you responsible for these lies?'

Alison rolled her eyes. 'No, Sep. I told you. We're studying the Tudors and Stuarts. That's what my notes were about, not the history of Theromantia. I'd never even heard of the place before yesterday, for crying out loud. It's reality regrowth, just like our Travelcards.'

The wizard continued to look at her suspiciously. 'It's your handwriting.'

Alison couldn't deny it. It was her handwriting, and it made her feel frightened to look at it – like glancing in a shop window and seeing a stranger's face looking out of the glass. It was her very own handwriting, and nobody had the right to hijack it to convey ideas that weren't hers. 'I didn't write it, Sep, honestly. What's all the fuss about, anyway?'

'It is a very grave matter to publish falsehoods about our past. Whoever did it will find themselves in serious trouble.'

'If they're trapped here, they're in serious trouble already,' she snapped. 'For heaven's sake, Sep, pull yourself together. You can't really think I wrote all that since yesterday evening! What on earth do you think I am?'

The wizard looked at her steadily for a moment. 'I'm not sure I know any more. I'd like to see the card you found in your bag.'

The card was still in her hand. After a moment's hesitation, she held it out. 'All right. I'm not trying to hide anything,' she said with a trace of defiance. 'But it's not mine. And if you look at it, you ought to see Kevin's card too.' She looked challengingly at Kevin.

Kevin wavered. Much as he would have liked to see Alison's photo, he didn't feel ready for a wider public showing of his own. 'We should wait for Mr Dempsey and the rest,' he said at last, sliding the gold card into his trouser pocket. Alison made a snorting sound that indicated what she felt about this suggestion. 'Reality regrowth's going to be affecting them too, isn't it?' he said defensively. A thought struck him. 'What's keeping them anyway? They should have been here ages ago. They were only going round to check the doors were locked.'

'Maybe something's come up.' To her own ears, her voice sounded thin and unconvincing.

'Like what?'

It wasn't a shortage of possibilities that kept Alison from answering, but the sound of footsteps approaching along the corridor. She edged closer to the others. 'I don't know, but I think we're about to find out.'

Chapter Seven

Wizards are fascinated by abstract ideas and they don't care a fig for building regulations. As a result, Stolk Castle had developed over centuries into a structure of staggering complexity.

There were whole wings whose purpose had been so long forgotten that all they did was gather dust and spiders; corridors where silence lay so thick you could leave footprints in it. The areas in everyday use were only slightly less bewildering. Apprentices at Stolk Academy (on the third and fourth floors of the west wing) spent the first six weeks of their course getting to grips with castle geography, and during the whole of their first year they were advised at all times to carry a ball of string.

The hall where the Wizards' Council met was on the fifth floor of the tower, immediately below the landing-square. There, as darkness thickened into night, Catterat held an informal meeting.

It takes a lot to enrage a senior wizard, but being imprisoned in an alien world halfway up a mountain, tossed about by shifting realities, with no access to an interplanetary fax machine, will generally do the trick. The fate of Strepticon, who had been sent out on foot four hours earlier to explore and had not returned, weighed on them too. As Trebox said, it would be a dreadful thing if something had happened to the only person who could make sense of the council's accounts.

'His instructions were precise,' the Chief Wizard said thinly. 'All he had to do was find Similon, and he had his crystal to guide him. Like the missing agents, he has no excuse for failure. If he has failed, however, it makes our own attempt the more urgent.' He swivelled to look at Bloxifil, the acknowledged expert on carpet travel. 'Will it be safe to try again at dawn?'

A vision of their recent carpet flight rose up before Bloxifil's eyes. He groaned as the contents of his stomach rearranged themselves. 'It would be madness. We must wait for conditions to settle, and see what news Strepticon brings.'

'Kevin Son of Grork?' The stranger framed in the staffroom door was a large, solid man with a friendly face and a large knife in a sheath attached to a strap across his khaki jacket. He directed the inquiry to the company in general.

Out of the corner of his eye, Kevin saw Similon's lips part, and was spurred into speech. 'Never heard of him,' he said loudly.

'I'm afraid he's just popped out,' said Alison at the selfsame moment.

'Oh?' The stranger showed no apparent surprise at being handed two conflicting stories. Both Alison and Kevin regarded this as highly sinister.

'Turn left along the corridor, take the second flight of stairs on your right,' Alison persisted, 'then ask for the CDT room. That's where you'll find him. Isn't it?' she looked meaningfully at Kevin.

He swallowed and said quickly, 'Oh, *that* Kevin? I thought you meant someone else. Someone I'd never heard of.' He swallowed. 'If that's the Kevin you want, the one who went to the CDT room, then that's where he'll be. In the CDT room.' He looked desperately at Similon. 'That's right, isn't it, Sep?'

Similon looked mystified. 'Is this some kind of game? I thought you were—' He broke off, conscious that three pairs of eyes were gazing at him, one pair with mild interest, and the other two with something like anguish. He gave up. 'Look, if you don't mind, I'm going to read the rest of these.' He picked up Alison's ex-history notes. As he sat down on the couch, he added austerely, 'If you want my opinion, this hardly seems the time to play games. Some of us have more important matters to think about. But don't let me stop you.'

After this, neither Alison nor Kevin could think of anything at all to say. It fell to the newcomer to break the silence. 'Thanks, mate,' he said, addressing the back of Similon's head. 'Don't mind if I do come in, since I'm invited.' Before anyone could disabuse him of this misapprehension, he ambled in through the door, shutting it carefully behind him. 'The name's Yurt. I'll sit here and wait till Kev gets back. From wherever.'

'If it's him you want,' said Alison, still trying. 'He might be the wrong person, after all. You know, I'd look somewhere else if I were you.'

Yurt perched on the edge of the staffroom table. 'Nah. I don't fancy no more wandering about. Bad enough finding this place to start with. And there's some funny stuff going down out there.' He lowered his voice to a whisper. 'Your headmaster's having a bit of a barney with a wizard, and it looked to me like it could turn nasty. Tell you the truth, I'll be glad to get young Kev back where he belongs.'

'Where does he belong?' asked Kevin, trying to sound casual.

The stranger didn't seem to hear. He was looking speculatively at Alison. 'Haven't I seen you before somewheres? You got a familiar look to you. You a model?'

Regarding him with slightly more warmth, she shook her head again.

'I'm almost sure I seen a big picture of you some place. Not long ago, neither. I never forget a face.'

Kevin gave a loud cough. 'This Kevin Son of Grork,' he said insistently, 'why are you looking for him?' Yurt emerged from his trance and turned a limpid gaze upon him. Kevin shifted uneasily from foot to foot. 'Is he in trouble or what?'

'Trouble?' This suggestion seemed to strike the stranger as hugely entertaining. 'Kev? Whatever give you that idea? The Son of Grork ain't in trouble, mate. He'll make trouble, maybe, if he's a chip off the old block, but nobody's going to go making trouble for him. Not if they know what's good for them. Specially,' he gave a cheerful grin, 'not now.'

Kevin retreated into worried silence as he digested this information, leaving Alison to ask baldly, 'Why not?'

'He's had a bit of luck, ain't he? It ain't public yet, but between you and me, his uncle's died. Not to mention his cousins, his granpa, and just about every other Grork you like to mention. One of them accidents with dynamite seemingly, as happens in the best of fambleys. And what it means is—' he gave an artless smile, 'all of a sudden young Kev's number one Grork. Nacherly his granny wants him home quick sharp. To make sure he don't go having no tragic accident too, if you get my drift. You all right, mate?' he looked at Kevin kindly. 'You gone all green and wobbly. Have a sit-down.'

While Kevin tottered over to a chair, Alison concentrated on extracting further details, which their visitor seemed only too willing to supply. The picture that emerged was not exactly reassuring.

According to Yurt, the Grorks were a family of great power and influence – a load of gangsters, Kevin privately translated – who had run Theromantia on the quiet for centuries. You wanted something done? You asked a Grork to arrange it. You didn't want something done? They could arrange that too.

'How, exactly?' Alison asked. Yurt only tapped his nose and winked. She took this to mean that the Grorks' methods were a professional secret.

Naturally their power had aroused the envy of small-minded people, and as a result the family had had its share of tragedies. Kevin's own father, for instance, had apparently been struck down in his prime by a head cold brought on by a dip in the ocean with his feet in a block of cement. The day after the funeral, little Kevin's gran had packed him off to boarding-school, where he had spent the next ten years entirely forgotten by his family. It had taken the dynamite to jog the old lady's memory.

'And now she wants her little lad home,' Yurt finished cheerfully. 'To be a prop in her old age and polish off the Plurgs for her.'

Kevin's mouth felt dry. He moistened his lips and managed to ask, 'The Plurgs?'

'The lot who supplied the dynamite.' Yurt shook his head admiringly. 'A rare old character is Kev's gran. Not many her age – man *or* woman – could bring down a Plurg with a knife in the back at thirty paces like I seen her do. I wouldn't like to cross her, make no mistake. Which is why—' he swung himself off the table, ambled over to where Kevin was sitting and took him by the arm in a friendly fashion, 'you and me better get a move on. She's not a woman as likes to be kept waiting.'

Kevin found himself on his feet and moving, without in the least meaning to, towards the door.

He fought to free himself but fingers gripping him might as well have been iron bands. 'No! You've made a mistake. I'm the wrong Kevin! Let me explain!'

'He's right! He's nothing to do with the Grorks.

88

He's not even from Theromantia!' With great presence of mind, Alison flung herself in front of the door. She had no illusions, however, about what would happen if it came to a struggle. 'Sep!' she yelled as the stranger bore down on her, hauling Kevin in his wake. 'Do something! For the love of Logios, *help*!'

This anguished shriek – the wording of which startled her as much as anyone – made Sep lift his head with a frown. On Yurt the effect was even more dramatic.

He stopped dead in his tracks. 'So it's like that is it?' he growled, his face unreadable. 'Now I know where it was I seen you.' Suddenly the hand that wasn't busy grasping Kevin was holding the hilt of a knife. He held it out in front of him as he advanced towards the door. 'There's WANTED posters up for you all over town. There's a lot of folks been wondering where you disappeared to. Get out my way quick or I might have to tell them – Zelda!'

Alison had roughly 2.85 seconds to decide what to do. She knew this without a shadow of doubt, and the fact that she did know it frightened her far more than the immediate danger. After all, there were twenty-nine methods of disposing of an armed assailant, at least three of which had a greater than eighty per cent chance of success in her current situation.

There she went again. How could a blameless fifth-former at Westleigh High possibly come by that information?

Only 1.32 seconds to impact.

Flexing muscles she didn't know she possessed, Alison instinctively assumed the stance known to students of the Punghalese school of martial arts as the enraged stag beetle. It seemed to give Yurt pause for thought, and she could see Kevin's eyes goggling at her in alarm. He'd probably never seen a girl preparing to perform the deadly manoeuvre of kha-ntar.

Alison wasn't surprised about that.

She'd never seen anyone perform it either. In fact, she'd never even heard of it until the term popped into her mind from nowhere.

'This is stupid,' she said uncertainly. 'My name isn't Zelda.' Three pairs of eyes continued to regard her with alarm, suspicion, and – in the case of Yurt – open hostility. 'For the love of Logios,' she cried, 'why don't you believe me?'

Before anyone had a chance to answer, the door behind her flew open. Alison was catapulted to one side as the room filled with noise and shouting. Above the babble she heard a familiar voice bellow, 'This is outrageous! I don't care who you claim to be – you have no authority here! You will leave my school at once!'

Snatching a quick glance upwards, she caught sight of Mr Dempsey engaged in some kind of wrestling match with a tall, dark wizard. How she knew he was a wizard was a mystery, but once again, she hadn't a shadow of doubt. His arrival was almost certainly bad news for Sep, and quite possibly for her too, if he started getting her mixed up with Zelda like everyone else. Maybe Mr Dempsey would manage to sort things out. Until he did, the sensible plan appeared to be to retreat behind the sofa, and skulk there until further notice.

And if Zelda whoever-she-was wouldn't be seen dead hiding behind a sofa, so much the better. It should show even the stupidest person present – she was prepared to keep an open mind about who this was, but Kevin, Sep and Yurt were currently the front-runners – that she and the other girl had nothing in common.

Unfortunately, Alison's plan had a flaw, as she discovered when she rounded the corner of the sofa. There was no room to hide, because the space was already taken.

Sep had ducked down behind the sofa as soon as he recognised Strepticon. It was not in the finest traditions of wizardhood to hide, exactly, but he fully intended to come out in due course. Instinct told him that his senior colleague was not going to give him a fair hearing while having his leg bitten by an over-excited schoolchild. When tempers had cooled and the time was right, he would stand up and quietly and calmly explain what had gone wrong.

Strepticon would understand. As wizards went, the Council Treasurer was a sensible man.

Similon peered round the end of the sofa. The sensible man was trying to brain Mr Dempsey with a lump of crystal.

He inched softly backwards into the shadows. Better leave it a while. Stay out of sight and keep really quiet . . .

At this critical moment a voice behind him whispered 'Sep!' and a hand closed round his ankle.

It wasn't so much the fact that Similon screamed and sprang to his feet that spelled disaster as the fact that he did so during a temporary lull in the shouting. Every head swivelled in his direction, including that of Strepticon.

Similon froze in horror.

'Ha!' The Council Treasurer let go abruptly of Mr Dempsey's collar. 'At last – the traitor I seek! Septimus Similon, I arrest you in the name of the Wizards' Council.'

'Gibberish!' Mr Dempsey snapped. 'If you imagine for one moment that I will allow a madman to walk in here off the street and start arresting people, think again!'

A ragged cheer went up from several children, but it died away as Strepticon rounded upon the headmaster. 'Do not be so rash as to hinder me, Zlot,' he snarled. 'You will not be pardoned twice.'

'I am not—' Mr Dempsey began, in vain.

'You will shelter neither this traitor, nor that misguided creature whom you incited to rebellion. She will be hunted down!' Strepticon thundered. 'She will be dealt with! She will answer for her crimes! There is no hiding place in all of Theromantia for the rebel known as Zelda!'

Wriggling as far as she could underneath the sofa, Alison hoped with all her heart he was wrong.

And what with one thing and another, no one asked themselves what had become of Kevin.

Chapter Eight

Catterat, Chief Wizard of Theromantia, looked bleakly out from the battlements of Stolk Castle. The wizards' situation was not promising. They were in the wrong dimension, halfway up a wolf-infested mountain. Unless they wanted to starve, they were going to have to find a new place to live.

He went downstairs and called an urgent meeting.

'I see that we can't stay here, but why not just go home?' This timid question came from a dishevelled wizard with grey hair, who ought to have known better.

Catterat counted to ten in Universal, and then said with restraint, 'We will return to Theromantia at the appropriate moment. In the meantime, you may be glad to hear that a carrier-pigeon has arrived from Strepticon. He has apprehended Similon at Westleigh High School, which lies approximately two miles southwest. He describes it as a large building, poorly equipped in respect of dungeons but otherwise enjoying ample facilities. I propose that we adopt it as our headquarters in exile, and proceed there forthwith.'

There was a buzz of approval, which lasted about as long as it took people to grasp that they wouldn't be travelling by carpet. Wizards can walk – they have been known to travel as much as a furlong in a single day, over flat ground in fine weather – but two miles over difficult country was a very different matter.

The gathering broke up amid general gloom as each wizard went to pack an overnight bag.

As he made his way down three staircases, through endless corridor, and along a short tunnel to join the party in the main entrance hall, Catterat hoped that Westleigh High would prove an agreeable headquarters. It struck him as distinctly possible that they were going to be there for some time.

The wizards trooped out blinking into the winter

sunlight. A murmur of alarm broke from several when they saw the descent that lay ahead. As Catterat led the way down the slope, he congratulated himself on an earlier decision.

Morale was dangerously low already. He'd been right not to mention the wolves.

If Kevin Son of Grork had been expecting a rousing welcome, he was quickly disillusioned. His grandmother looked him up and down, winced, and said, 'Yes. Well. That school has a lot to answer for, but I daresay it's not too late. What can you do with a knife?'

Open a letter? Carve his initials on the window-sill? Instinct told Kevin these were not the answers she was waiting for. He fell back on the truth. 'I am not Kevin Son of Grork,' he said. 'I'm Kevin Young, and I live in Axborough.'

The wizened face brightened. 'Ah, they taught you that much, anyway. You lie very nicely, very nicely indeed. We'll make something of you yet. Show him his room, Sergeant. He'll feel better when he's had a lie-down.'

'I may feel better,' Kevin said with dignity, 'but I still won't be called Grork. I want to go home.'

His grandmother gave his arm a pat. 'I know, I know. Your father was the same. Not sixteen, and wanting to set up house with your mum, never mind he had to build up a business, and her with her career to think of. I told him straight, a girl doesn't get to be number one assassin these days without she keeps her mind on her work. The competition's killing. He wouldn't listen to me, but I'm not going to let you make the same mistake.'

'I don't know what you're talking about,' said Kevin with some heat. Experience of his own gran back home suggested she was about to become seriously embarrassing.

'I know all about this Zelda,' she said, proving his instincts right, 'and believe you me, lovey, it won't work.'

Kevin felt a wave of colour creep up his neck. 'Look,' he said pugnaciously, 'just wait a minute. You've got this all wrong.'

She shook her head. 'You're the one what's wrong, grandson. I seen it too many times before. Fresh out of school. Think you know it all. Your Zelda's in a different league from that. No one tops the Wanted lists in five dimensions by being soft and cuddly, no matter what story she told you. She's serious trouble is Zelda Plurg.'

'Zelda *Plurg*?' exclaimed Kevin. Even in the midst of his own troubles he had time to feel sorry for Alison. It was bad enough everyone thinking he was the Son of Grork, but at least he didn't have to come to terms with being Public Enemy Number One. 'I never knew that was her last name.'

'Didn't think so,' said his grandmother with satisfaction. 'I wouldn't be surprised if there was a few other little things she forgot to mention too. Like how she got that Zlot to spill the wizards' secrets. And how she tried to use them herself, against all laws of nature. Take my word for it, Kev, you've had a lucky escape. Now, off you go and rest. There's a delegation of grave-diggers due at midday, and you'll be representing the family interests.'

'I'll be what?' Kevin shied away in alarm, but Yurt's fingers fastened round his arm once more. 'Look, Gran, I keep telling you – you're making a mis—'

The struggle he put up made not the least difference. As she waved him goodbye, the Mother of Grork added another item to her mental list of areas in which her grandson needed training.

Wrestling.

A boy shouldn't rely on his knife. Particularly a boy as slow to make use of it as Kevin. It made her wonder why she'd been paying Zlot's fees for ten years when her grandson came home in that condition. Best get him some professional instruction.

She reached for her pen and dashed off a memo to Yurt to present himself at three o'clock to give Kevin his first lesson. She signed her name with a

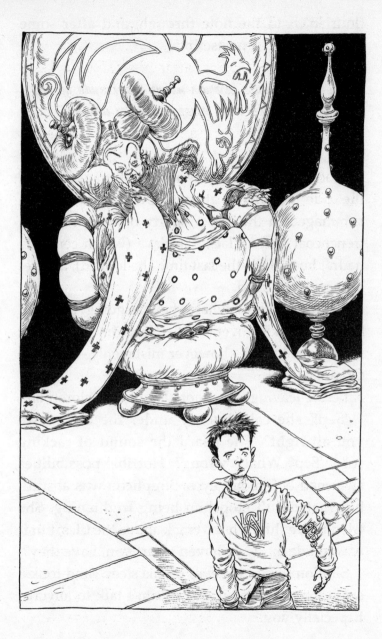

flourish, read the note through, and after some thought added a postscript:

PF: Yt wd knotte furpryse me yf you fownde ye boy fomewhat unfytte. Pray bringe ye fmaller alligator.

At noon, obeying a mysterious rhythm of its own, the tide withdrew at last. Once again Alison rummaged in the lost property box, fished out a trenchcoat and a black balaclava (which certainly hadn't been there the last time she looked), and set off across the sand.

She didn't know where she was going, but with Strepticon taking over, Westleigh High was no place for anyone linked – however mistakenly – with the Organisation.

Before leaving, she crept along to the storeroom.

'Sep!' she called softly under the door. 'Are you all right?' She heard the sound of racking sobs. 'Sep? What's wrong?' Horrible possibilities swarmed before her eyes. Strepticon was absurd, but that didn't stop him being frightening. She tried to see through the crack above the tiles, but it was too dark. 'They haven't hurt you, have they?'

Similon wiped his eyes on his sleeve and took a shaky breath. 'Go away. I mustn't talk to anyone. Especially you.'

'Oh, Sep!' For a moment Alison felt like crying herself. 'I'm not Zelda. I'm Alison, and I want to help. I'll see if I can find the caretaker's spare key.'

'Don't bother,' he said listlessly. 'Do you think I'd trust you even if you found it? You must take me for as big a fool as Zlot. I am a wizard. I will stand trial before my peers.'

'They'll find you guilty!' Alison cried. 'You know they will!'

'They might not. Anyway, I shall abide by their verdict. Go away, or – or I'll shout for Strepticon,' he finished wildly.

'You wouldn't!'

'If you don't go, I'll have no choice.'

Alison swallowed hard. 'If that's what you want,' she said at last. 'Goodbye, Sep. I . . . I hope things turn out well. At the trial, I mean. And I'm sorry I said it was all your fault. Even though it was. I shouldn't have said it. I'm sorry.'

She lingered as long as she dared, hoping for an answer, but all she heard was Strepticon's voice barking an order. There was nothing for it but to scramble to her feet and slip away.

Soon the school dropped out of sight behind her. To her right, wet sand stretched down to the water's edge; to her left, small dunes had risen overnight. The school playing fields must lie beneath them somewhere, but if she hadn't known this, she would never have guessed. Thin clusters of marram grass had sprung up here and there. She had the strange feeling that if she stopped for a moment, she would be able to hear the network of roots spreading, the tiny pop as each fresh blade emerged from the sand.

Grass, sand, waves . . . everything around her was less than forty-eight hours old, but it looked as if it had been there for ever. She picked her way past piles of litter scattered along the hightide mark, fascinated to see the debris stranded there: a gym shoe with no laces, a small drowned dragon, half an orange, a green bottle (still corked) with what looked like a rolled sheet of paper inside.

Alison frowned and stooped.

It was a sheet of paper, all right, with something written on it. It was curled up too tightly for her to be able to read through the glass, but the fact that someone had bothered to put it in there at all made her think it must be important.

The cork was wedged too deep in the neck of the bottle for her fingers to find a grip, so she cracked the neck hard against a stone and picked the scroll out from among the splinters. It began boldly:

Do you hate wizards?

Do you despise the silly way they talk and the awful clothes they wear? Do you loathe the way they act as if they are the only ones who know anything? Do you wish they would just occasionally wash their socks?

Cheer up! You are not alone! Each and every member of the Organisation feels the same! Join us and strike a blow for a cleaner, better Theromantia.

Find out more about the Organisation by visiting its headquarters (second left behind the Green Parrot) during office hours: Mon-Thurs, 2–5pm.

PS Females only accepted as full members.
PPS Payment of a fee entitles males to help with tea and washing up.

DOWN WITH THE WIZARDS!

Alison read this notice twice. When she had folded it carefully and placed it inside her coat pocket, she went on her way with new zing in her stride.

Where better to take refuge than with an organisation dedicated to fighting the wizards? If she told them how the council was hunting her, surely they'd take her in. Maybe she'd find the real Zelda there, and be able to clear up the confusion over who she was! All she had to do was find the Green Parrot before the wizards found her.

Find the Green Parrot? something inside her said. *Surely you remember? You face the castle flagpole, turn ninety degrees to the left, and take the road past the apothecary's store.*

As she trudged up a sand-dune in order to scan the horizon, Alison tried to remember who had given her these directions. 'It must have been Sep, or Fentwick,' she said aloud. 'I'm sure it wasn't Zlot or Strepticon. Mr Dempsey or Strepticon, I should say.'

She frowned. The slip of the tongue was strangely unnerving. 'It was Fentwick who told me the way,' she told a seagull with great firmness. As it waddled away across the sand, she called after it, 'I remember him telling me now. I remember distinctly.'

The trouble was, she didn't. The directions were just there, the way the instructions on martial arts had been.

It was reality regrowth again, taking place inside her own head.

Feeling rather sick, she faced the flagpole and turned ninety degrees to the left.

Chapter Nine

Forty wizards and twenty-six apprentices set out from Stolk Castle. Twenty-three wizards, eight apprentices and one giant anteater reached their destination. They arrived at Westleigh High tired, frightened, hungry, and in the case of the anteater, in a state of shock, but at least they were alive. This was more than could be said for many. The slow had suffered terribly from the wolves; those in bright clothes had been singled out by the thelamungus; Helibron had wandered over the edge of a precipice; Nebukar sank in a patch of quicksand, refusing to grasp Trebok's staff because that would have meant dropping his crystal; most of the apprentices had somehow melted away in the forest.

And then there was Bloxifil.

Catterat glowered at the anteater. 'You were warned, like everyone: no magic. You knew the risks, and yet you disobeyed. Explain yourself.'

The anteater gave a long, complicated whine.

'That is no excuse,' the Chief Wizard snapped. 'How would it be if we all broke the rules whenever we saw a wolf? To use magic with reality in flux – you, a member of Council! Anything could have happened! It is fortunate that the outcome was not far worse, for all of us. Future mistakes may not end so happily. I will have a good deal more to say on this subject once I have dealt with Similon.'

He swept off with Bloxifil shuffling at his heels.

In theory, fearful formalities surround a wizard's trial. Every detail, from where people sit to the way the Chief Wizard laces his boots, is laid down at mind-numbing length in records that pre-date Logios. In practice, Chief Wizards consider themselves free to make cuts as and when the occasion demands. Thus, when Similon limped into the school assembly hall to face twenty-four surviving colleagues and one anteater, Catterat opened by announcing: 'This is the trial of Septimus Similon, wizard fourth class. Prisoner, do you admit you are this traitor?'

After the gloom of the storeroom, the sunlight streaming through the high windows hurt Similon's eyes. His wrists and ankles hurt too, where the skipping ropes had chafed them. But these discomforts were nothing compared with the pain in his heart. One glance at Catterat's face told him his plight was every bit as bad as he'd feared. The battle-scarred wooden floor seemed a far more friendly place to look. 'I am Septimus Similon,' he said sadly. 'But—'

'Silence!' Catterat snapped. 'Treasurer, read the charges.'

Strepticon rose and cleared his throat. 'Septimus Similon, you are charged that on the forty-fourth day of the month of Rabilhar you did, stupidly and with absolutely no forethought, refute the thirty-ninth theorem of Logios the Great, and in so doing did injure the fabric of reality in two dimensions, causing extreme inconvenience to fellow wizards. Furthermore . . .'

Strepticon's experience of public speaking was limited to reciting balance sheets at council meetings, and he saw no need to adjust his style for a charge sheet that ran to a mere ten pages. After five minutes even Similon had lost the will to listen, while those in the audience who were still awake chatted among themselves. This peaceful state was shattered by a shout of 'Rubbish!' from the back of the hall.

'What?' the Treasurer asked, momentarily flustered.

'I said "Rubbish!" ' A tall figure strode up the aisle. 'Call this a trial?' Mr Dempsey, alias the evil Zlot, demanded with a snort of contempt.

Similon gave a bleat of horror.

'It *is* a trial,' said Catterat, white with fury. 'And you have no business here. Leave my council chamber!'

'Leave my assembly hall!' ordered Mr Dempsey in return. 'I have explained the position several times to your underling –' he pointed at Strepticon, who bristled with indignation '– but he seems extraordinarily stupid. I intend to take legal action to have you expelled at the first opportunity and, in the meantime, I refuse to stand by and witness this mockery of justice.' The headmaster flung out a hand towards Similon. 'Where is this man's lawyer? Who has been appointed to speak up for him? No one? Then it's not a trial. You've found him guilty before you start.'

This was quite true, and quite normal for Theromantia, but Catterat was not about to say so. His glare, which could shrivel Similon like a blowtorch, had no visible effect on his oldest enemy. 'Does the prisoner wish for a lawyer?' the Chief Wizard asked at last, his eyes not leaving the headmaster's face.

'Of course he does!'

'No, I don't!' Similon's cry of alarm came too late.

'Whom does he wish to have as his lawyer?' Catterat asked with a degree of menace that added to Similon's panic.

'I don't want anyone!' Aware that any chance of acquittal was vanishing before his eyes, Similon made the mistake of trying to leap to his feet, only to discover that after twenty-four hours in the store-room, his legs refused to obey orders. As the parquet flooring rushed up to meet him, he heard the renegade Zlot proclaim, 'I will be his lawyer,' in ringing tones.

'That's it, then,' was his last conscious thought. 'I'm finished.'

Luckily for a fugitive from justice, there were other routes to Organisation HQ than the public approach outlined in the message in the bottle, and luckily for Alison, she seemed familiar with most of them.

As she shinned up a drainpipe, ran lightly along a flat roof, and jumped down on to a ripe manure heap, it did cross her mind to wonder how she knew what to do with such certainty, but she was too busy surviving to worry about anything else.

However, when she arrived on the Organisation's doorstep, breathless and reeking of horse dung, the certainty that had stood her in such good stead suddenly vanished. It was all very well for the notice on the door to proclaim, as it did:

All genuine callers welcome!
Come in and join the struggle!
The Organisation needs YOU!

How were the genuine callers meant to the react to the card pinned beneath, with its rather different message?

Members only
Trespassers will be PERSECUTED
This means YOU

She felt quite persecuted enough already, thank you, without taking on the Organisation. On the other hand, where else could she go if not to the one group who seemed prepared to take on the wizards? Who else in Axborough or Theromantia was likely to shelter her?

She reached for the iron knocker.

The knock had hardly died away when a small grille sprang open halfway up the door. 'I warn you,' said a disembodied voice, 'there are twenty-six of us here, armed to the teeth and ready to give our lives for the cause.'

Good news though this was from one standpoint, it was rather alarming from another. Alison cleared her throat and said nervously, 'I've come to join the Organisation. The wizards are after me.'

She might as well have said nothing.

'There are dogs too. They haven't eaten anyone since Wednesday, so they're absolutely ravenous. I'm letting them off their chains now.'

'Please don't! All I want to do is—' Her attempt to explain was interrupted by loud clanks and a series of bloodthirsty growls.

'Down, Fang,' said the voice breathlessly. 'Stop that, Butcher. You don't attack till *I* say.' More clanks, a snarl and a yelp.

Suddenly enraged, Alison seized the knocker and hammered furiously on the door. 'You have to let me in – there's nowhere else I can go!' she cried. 'How can you expect people to join if all you do is tell them to go away? It's completely illogical!'

The door opened a crack. 'Logic isn't everything, you know.' The unseen speaker sounded unruffled. 'What's the password?'

'How should I know?' Exasperation was rapidly becoming Alison's strongest emotion. 'I'm not a member yet! Are members the only ones who are allowed to become members? Because if so, you're not going to get anywhere.'

The crack widened. 'We don't want people who are afraid of contradictions,' the voice informed her. It continued less loftily, 'There isn't a password, as a matter of fact. Or if there is one, nobody's told me. They went off in a terrible hurry, you see.'

The last words tumbled out in a rush, so that Alison had difficulty catching them, and they seemed to come from lower down than she would have expected. If it hadn't been for the dogs, she'd have sneaked a look round the door. 'Who went off?'

'All of them. They said they were going to find Zelda, and I was to stay here till they came back, only they haven't. And it's almost three days.' Alison guessed that the unseen speaker's airy tone was achieved at some cost. 'And the wizards have been at it again, because everything's changed outside. I hate it when that happens.'

Alison nodded, knowing exactly what she meant. 'So do I,' she said with feeling.

'And I hope they come back soon, because I've got a very important prisoner. I'm Mave. You can come in if you want,' the voice finished casually.

Alison put one hand on the door. 'Where are the dogs?'

'There aren't any really. Just me. And the prisoner,

112

of course. Not that he's much help. He makes horrible tea, and I had to show him how to wash up last night. And he calls himself a professor!'

'A professor?' Alison jumped. 'A professor of wizardry?'

'That's what he says. Anyway, I had to hit him with a saucepan or he might have escaped. Wizards are always escaping.'

The door swung open, revealing a thin red-headed girl with spectacles, who looked about ten years old. She was brandishing a large saucepan with a dent in one side, and something in her face suggested to Alison that she was quite prepared to use this on her, or anyone else who showed signs of giving trouble.

But as Alison stepped cautiously inside, the grim expression wavered. Disbelief, doubt and hope flickered across the girl's face, before they gave way to recognition and relief.

'Zelda!' The saucepan was cast aside as Mave flung herself forward. 'Why didn't you say! I almost didn't recognise you! You've come back!'

Like many another wizard, Similon had secretly dreamed of being asked to address a large assembly. He had imagined standing before them, wearing a purple cloak trimmed with sable. He saw himself, modest but confident, holding the gathering in the palm of his hand. Never in his worst nightmare had he envisaged a scene like this.

The only ally he had in the whole hall was a renegade wizard whose support was going to double his sentence.

'Go on,' his self-appointed lawyer hissed. 'Tell them what you were trying to do. Make them understand what happened.'

As if anyone could . . .

Even to his own ears, Similon's explanation sounded limp and unconvincing – yet it was true, every word of it.

'I didn't mean any harm,' he finished with a flicker of spirit. 'If Logios had said you could enclose a big area, I wouldn't have tried to. I wanted to prove something wrong, and it happened to be Theorem 39, that's all.'

'Logios said it couldn't be done because it shouldn't be done,' Catterat said, drumming his fingers. 'Didn't your tutors ever tell you that enclosed spaces are highly unpredictable? Far finer wizards than you have spent their whole lives studying them without reaching any conclusion. This is as it should be. The potential consequences of theromantic enclosure are immense. Did you consider, for example, how your barrier –' Catterat pronounced the word with scorn '– would affect distancing spells?'

Similon looked miserable. 'I'm afraid I didn't think about—'

'Spells of substitution?' snapped Strepticon.

'I don't—'

'What about propulsive and repulsive motion? Gravitational reversement? Simplary requestion?'

Similon gave up trying to answer.

'What about the annual convention?' someone asked from the floor. 'It's next month in Uticon. We've made a block booking. How are we meant to get there?'

Several voices murmured agreement. 'The tickets cost fifty ducats.'

'And then there's accommodation.'

'I had my cloak cleaned specially. That's another twelve ducats.'

Mr Dempsey rose to his feet. 'I object. My client can hardly be held responsible for the financial consequences of decisions to which he was not a party.'

It was apparent that the Chief Wizard's patience was wearing thin. 'Of course he can! Sit down and be quiet! I have heard enough.' He glared at Similon. 'The prisoner will rise to hear the court's verdict.'

'I object,' said Mr Dempsey, for the eighth and last time. Exasperated beyond endurance, Catterat forgot his own ban on magic and snapped his fingers.

The digital enchantment he was aiming for was the kind of thing apprentices learn in their first year at Stolk Academy, a simple spell of tongue binding to enforce silence. Once again, with reality in flux, the consequences were unexpected. When the thick smoke cleared, there on the floor where Mr Dempsey had stood was a small grey hamster.

Catterat was the first to recover his voice. 'Make a note,' he told Strepticon calmly. 'Enclosure seems to reduce the number of variables we have to allow for in spells of transformation. Most promising. The sooner we start a series of controlled experiments the better. As for you—' he raised his eyes from the hamster to the unhappy figure of Similon, and his voice sharpened. 'This court finds you guilty of conduct unbecoming a wizard and of having brought your profession into disrepute. You are stripped of your rank, and cast out from the fellowship of wizards for ever.'

'Cast out?' Similon whispered. 'But that's what I am – a wizard. If I'm not that, I'm nothing.'

'Quite,' said Catterat coolly. 'And as nothing, may I remind you that you no longer have a place here?'

The walk to the door of the hall seemed the longest Similon had ever taken, and the loneliest. Nobody spoke up to wish him luck. No hand reached out to shake his own. The men he knew, the wizards he had trained beside, watched him go in silence, without sorrow and without spite.

How could he blame them? He would have done the same himself.

Outside in the sandy playground, he shut his eyes and leaned his head against the wall. 'I am alone,' he said – which was not, strictly speaking, accurate.

As he stumbled towards the dunes, the grey hamster that clung grimly to the cuff of his trousers began to inch its way up the thick cloth towards the safety of the ex-wizard's pocket.

'In you go, lad,' said Yurt. Kevin reeled as the sergeant's encouraging pat flattened him against the wall of the alligator pen. 'The trick is, don't let 'em know you're scared. They smell fear, alligators do, and when they smell it . . .' He sucked his breath in through the gap where his front teeth should have been, and expelled it again with a loud pop.

Kevin swallowed. 'Then what?' Like its master, the alligator was missing its front teeth but its jaws looked as if they could crack bones like matchsticks. It glared up at Kevin from its pen, breathing heavily through its mouth.

'They go bananas,' the sergeant replied cheerfully. 'What you waiting for, lad? Want a leg-up?'

If anyone had asked Kevin before that moment what his worst experience was so far, he'd have said it was the games period when the captain of the football team pleaded to be allowed to play a man short rather than have Kevin on his side, but this was worse, far worse. Yurt's arms, helpfully outstretched, were like tree-trunks. Any second now they were going to fasten themselves round Kevin's knees and toss him to the alligator.

The thought of what would happen then made the bones in Kevin's legs go soft, and a swishing sound fill his ears. Was he, for the first time in his life, about to faint? He shut his eyes hopefully and waited, but instead of a black tide sweeping over him, he felt the sergeant's fingers close around his ankle.

'Wait! Let's talk about this,' Kevin said, to his own surprise.

Yurt's grip tightened. 'What's there to talk about?'

Kevin registered that this was a good question. Apart from his mind being a total blank, he was so panicked that he couldn't have said a word to save his life. It was therefore with some astonishment that he heard himself saying, 'Plenty. I've got a proposition for you, Sergeant.'

'Oh yeah?' Kevin's feet were already off the ground, his hands clinging grimly to the side of the alligator-pen, when Yurt paused. 'What proposition would that be, laddie?'

Ten thousand, said a stranger inside Kevin's head.

'Ten thousand,' said Kevin.

Ten thousand what, for heaven's sake?

'Twenty,' said Yurt.

He seemed to know what they were talking about. Nice someone did. Twenty it was, then. With a surge of relief, Kevin opened his mouth to say Done, and heard instead, Eleven . . .

'Eleven thousand,' he heard himself say.

Oh no.

'Nineteen.'

'Twelve and a half.'

'Seventeen fifty.'

'Ten tomorrow, and three later.' This was ridiculous. Kevin could feel beads of sweat popping up on his forehead, which was still at an angle of ninety degrees to the ground.

'Fifteen now, and two more Thursday week.'

Out of the corner of one eye Kevin could see the alligator dribbling. A nasty little puddle had formed between its two front feet. 'Nine the day after tomorrow, and five more a fortnight yesterday,' he cried. 'That's my final offer.'

The world somersaulted back to its normal position. For a split second his feet landed on the ground, and then one of the tree-trunk arms gave him a buffet that flattened him against the alligator-pen for the second time. 'Done!' Yurt chortled, whipping a scroll and pen from his jacket pocket. 'Sign here to make it legal.'

The scroll was covered with purple hieroglyphics. Kevin looked at them with mistrust. 'What does it say? I can't read a word of it.'

'Lawyers' talk,' said Yurt easily. 'Don't worry about it, lad.' As Kevin continued to hesitate, he reached out a friendly hand for the boy's elbow, and administered a squeeze that almost sent him into orbit. 'Of course, if signing's a problem, we can always go ahead with the wrestling. That's what your granny wants, after all.'

Kevin's hand flew to the pen. A second later Yurt beamed and tucked the scroll away.

'Right! That's settled. The first instalment of nine thousand ducats comes due the day after tomorrow. I'll bring the cart along at noon to pick it up.'

Ducats? Kevin's knees buckled. Nine thousand ducats? How on earth was he going to get out of that?

You bag the ducats up, of course, whispered his inner voice. *Only it's not ducats you put in the bags. It's easy. Wait and see.*

'Right,' said Kevin faintly.

Yurt beamed. 'And don't bother to bag it up, like your dad always used to. You'd never believe the things that find their way into bags of ducats sometimes: scraps of iron, old bottle-tops, rusty counters . . .' He tapped Kevin gently on the chest, depriving him for a moment of breath. 'When it comes to ducats, son, my advice is do as I do: count 'em one by one, and count 'em yourself.'

Kevin waited for his inner voice to tell him the way out of that one. Unfortunately it had switched off.

Chapter Ten

Where can a wizard go when he's no longer a wizard?

Nowhere.

When you have lost everything that made you who you were, there is nowhere, in any dimension, that makes sense to go.

Similon's feet carried him over the sand, across the dunes and through the busy streets of Stolk. Deaf and blind to everything except his own pain, he saw nothing and heard nothing on the way. He didn't see afternoon fade to twilight, or dusk thicken to night. The first time he even registered that it was dark was when he crashed head first into something large and solid blocking his path.

Despair is one thing, but a sharp blow on the forehead is in a class of its own. Similon doubled up, clutching his head, and uttered several phrases wizards aren't meant to use when anyone can hear them. At that point he remembered that it didn't matter who overheard, because he wasn't a wizard any longer.

'Newts and toads!' he said defiantly. 'Vipers! What a frog of a place to leave a statue.'

This was hardly fair, given that the statue of Logios on which he had nearly brained himself stood in the middle of Stolk's largest square and was the best-known landmark in Theromantia. Reaching out cautiously, Similon's fingers quivered as they touched the row of curved stones that ran along the top of the pedestal.

For the space of a heartbeat, his brain stopped working. When it came back to life, his hands skated blindly backwards and forwards over the line of gooves he had just discovered.

He was imagining things, he must be!

But he wasn't.

The letters cut into the stone pedestal no longer spelled out the name of the greatest of

Theromantian wizards. They spelled out – Similon groaned and slid to his knees – Alfred Baxtenbrat!

This had to be his fault too. Everything was his fault, from start to finish. His life was over, and there was no one to blame but himself.

When he recovered enough to fumble for his handkerchief, the hamster bit him on the finger.

Luckily for Alison, the last thing she expected was a peaceful night.

She had no bed or blankets.

She was sharing the Organisation's office not merely with Fentwick – in a foul mood that showed itself in angry muttering punctuated by snorts and grunts as he tried to bandage his head with a torn-up sheet – but with, of all things, Similon's cat.

'Don't ask me how the brute got here,' was Fentwick's response to a mild question. 'With the thelamungus snapping at my neck, and that idiot refusing to let me in without the password, it must have somehow slipped my mind that I was meant to be looking after a . . . a newting *cat*.'

The brute in question was curled up on the room's only chair, producing an occasional rumble that might have been a purr or a growl. In its own way it was as disturbing a room-mate as Fentwick.

If a further reason for staying awake were

needed, there was the fact that Alison wasn't sure she even wanted to sleep. What if, when she closed her eyes, Zelda's voice began to whisper?

'Just think!' she said to Fentwick during a lull in his grumbling, 'I might end up dreaming her dreams instead of my own!'

She tried to pass this off as a joke, but the truth was she didn't find it funny. From what she knew of Zelda, her dreams were sure to be nightmares.

Beyond giving a cross between a snarl and a grunt, Fentwick ignored this, so she drew her knees up under her chin and settled down to watch. He'd been rude when she offered to help him earlier – so rude, in fact, that there probably wasn't much wrong with him. Which was just as well, since the bandage sagged and looked set to fall off any minute.

'You don't need a bandage anyway. It's only a bruise.' Catching his eye, she conceded, 'All right. There's a bit of a bump, and a cut too. But it's nothing serious.'

'How would you know what's serious?' He gave the bandage a tug so violent he only narrowly escaped choking himself. When he'd recovered he went on: 'That wretched sister of yours could have killed me. And if she had, you know what would have happened?' He scowled furiously. 'I'd be dead! I need a doctor!'

'You know very well she's not my sister. She just thinks I'm Zelda.'

He finished coiling the bandage up and popped it in a pocket. 'Everyone seems to think you're Zelda.' This was true, but it didn't make Alison feel better. Nor did his next remark. 'I wonder where the silly girl is?'

Alison had been wondering this too. None of the possibilities struck her as encouraging. She stretched out her legs and studied her toes.

'I think she's outside the barrier. Maybe she'll never be able to get back.' Her eyes flew open wide as a new possibility struck her. 'Maybe something's happened to her. Maybe she's dead!'

He produced a special noise conveying scorn and impatience. 'If she were dead, you'd be someone else.' Seeing her blank face, he gave an exaggerated sigh. 'That's how reality adjustment works. You're Zelda because she ought to be here and she isn't. Does that help?'

'No,' she said in a tight voice. 'Not really. If you must know, it doesn't help one bit.'

'All right, look at it this way. Zelda's not being here when she ought to be means there's a . . . a vacancy for her in this dimension. You were there in the right place at the right time to fill it. If she were dead, there'd be no vacancy. Reality would have to make you someone else.'

'Someone else?' repeated Alison in outrage. 'What do you mean, "make me someone else"?'

He threw his hands in the air. 'It's perfectly simple to grasp if you put your mind to it.'

She jumped to her feet. 'Why can't I stay me? That's who I am. Why do I have to change at all?'

He gave his head a pitying shake. In some mysterious fashion, what he obviously saw as her extraordinary stupidity seemed to have cheered him up. 'Don't be obtuse. Alison belongs in another dimension. This is Theromantia, give or take a few minor details. The person you were—'

'Are!'

'The person you were has no home here. No family. No history. In short, no identity. She had to become someone else. So did Kevin, and all the other people trapped by Similon's antics in a world where they don't belong. That's obviously how reality sees it, in any case.' He beamed, completely restored to good humour. 'You might as well accept it. There's nothing to be done, until I sort things out.'

On the point of a heated denial that she could ever accept being Zelda, Alison stopped. Fentwick might be infuriating, but she had decided long ago that he was no fool. Could he really sort things out, and get everything back the way it used to be? It was almost more than she dared hope.

Wizards spend the fifth of their seven years of study learning how to lie convincingly to clients, and other people who don't count (that means everyone who isn't a wizard). Unlike Similon, who had failed this part of the course five times, Fentwick had scored a distinction.

'Of course I can do it,' he said gruffly. 'It's only a matter of time. What I need is an hour's peace to check a couple of references in the book I had the sense to bring along, then I can get cracking. Probably have everything straight by tomorrow.' A trace of acid crept back into his voice. 'I'm assuming you can persuade that terrorist not to knock me out again. Could you manage that, as a special favour? After all, I will be saving the dimension.'

'Of course!' Marvellously reassured, Alison hurried out to tell Mave their troubles should soon be over. The door-keeper was in the cellar, studying an enormous notebook by candlelight.

'What troubles?' she asked vaguely. When Alison reminded her, she shook her head. 'That? That doesn't matter any more. You're back, and we can start on Plan X right away.'

'Look, I keep telling you, I'm *not* Zelda. What's Plan X?' Alison looked at her with misgiving.

Mave flipped the notebook shut. 'I wish you'd stop pretending. It's a brilliant disguise, of course, but do you think I don't know my own sister? As for Plan X, the whole Organisation knows you made that up yourself. And it's going to end the power of the wizards for ever!'

Shortly before dawn Strepticon, answering a call of nature, discovered the council's greatest expert on plagues very dead in the junior cloakroom. Quivering from head to foot, he went to rouse Catterat, who had retired to bed on the staffroom floor.

'It must have been the thelamungus. It seems to have knocked its way in through the wall, and then—' he swallowed. He preferred not to think about what had happened to Trebok after that. 'The injuries are definitely the work of more than one beak, and when I found the right foot underneath the radiator, the angle of the lacerations . . .'

The Chief Wizard shut his ears. His rest had been broken by fractured dreams and – as the staffroom fire died – the deepening December chill. He'd been forced to rummage in a chest of clothes for something to wear to keep a spark of heat in his body. All he had found to fit him were a hat and an overall festooned with straps, which he had struggled into in the dark. He had spent the minutes before he nodded off trying to pin down just what it was they smelled of.

He touched the hat and the smell wafted out

again, dark green and soupy, with a hint of . . .
what?

Lungwort?

Catterat froze. The whisper seemed to come from inside his own skull, but he'd never seen a sprig of lungwort, let alone smelled one. He shook his head, and heard the disembodied voice again:

Oregano?

Was there such a thing?

Still turning a deaf ear to Strepticon, he rose and padded stiffly across to the window. With each stride, the hem of the overall swished against the back of his calves.

The Treasurer, in the middle of a meticulous description of a chunk of Trebok's lower intestine, gave a grunt of surprise.

The Chief Wizard was wearing an apron. Stranger still, he was wearing it back-to-front. The hat looked like the sort of thing kitchen workers wore. The whole outfit gave off an aroma that reminded him unpleasantly of the dining-hall. If he'd had to describe it, he would have said it was like elderly toad on the turn, mingled with a leg or two of squashed spider.

Catterat held the hat up to the light to sniff a dark, crusted stain near the brim. Something about the tilt of his head suggested to Strepticon that he was listening.

'Frumentary?'

Surprised, Strepticon glanced back over his shoulder to see if anyone else had come in. There was no one. Catterat seemed to be speaking to thin air.

'I don't think I . . .' Strepticon broke off as the Chief Wizard spun round to glare at a spot by his right ear.

'Speak up. If it's frogspawn, say so. What? Pickled mice? What do you mean, I should know?' With a sudden growl Catterat hurled the hat in the air and kicked it with controlled rage into the wastepaper bin in the farthest corner of the staffroom.

It was, by any standards, an extraordinary kick. Even more surprising to Strepticon was the fact that he knew this, and knew it because something told him. Literally.

While he was still trying to come to terms with this, his hands began to clap of their own accord, and a voice he barely recognised as his own cried boisterously, 'Bravo, Catters! Do that three times and I'll stand you a double elixir!

As soon as the words were out, he clapped a hand to his mouth in horror.

He'd called the Chief Wizard 'Catters'! Almost as bad, he'd offered to buy him a drink – Catterat, famous for never touching anything stronger than diluted extract of beetle! The best thing that could happen in the circumstances would be for the floor to open and swallow him up.

Nothing of the kind happened, however. In the end, Strepticon, very red in the face, looked up.

It's a grave breach of etiquette for two high-ranking wizards to look each other full in the eye, so when Catterat and Strepticon found themselves doing so, they coughed and immediately turned away. It was too late, however: that split second of eye-contact had been enough. It takes far less than a split second to see that someone is frightened.

Particularly when you're in the same state yourself.

Catterat stalked to the bin to retrieve his hat. Strepticon bustled across to the noticeboard by the door, his face as blank as if he were balancing accounts.

It didn't stay blank for long. As usual, the board was covered with notices. They looked quite normal, until you started to read them, as Strepticon did.

'Catters . . .' he exclaimed in a strangled voice a moment later. 'I mean, Catterat. Wh-what do you make of this?'

'This' was a bold announcement, smack in the middle of the board:

'Zlot? A professor?' Strepticon sounded as if he'd just been kicked in the stomach, which in a sense he had. His ambition was to be a professor himself. 'What does this mean? It can't be true, it can't!'

A chief wizard outranks a professor any day, but Catterat was equally appalled.

'That charlatan will be a professor,' he said icily, 'on the day that Baxtenbrat supplants Logios. In other words, never.' He elbowed Strepticon aside so that he could see the board properly. 'Don't stand gaping. There's no time to lose. What else has reality been up to while we were asleep? For the love of Logios!'

Immediately above the lecture advertisement was

a smaller, more discreet announcement:

> **Who will you be tomorrow?**
> **Ask Madame Vasari!**
> *Gaze into her crystal ball and see*
> ***all** the answers for*
> *only **10 ducats!***
> *Can you afford **not** to look?*

Fortune-telling of any kind is anathema to a wizard, but that wasn't what caused Catterat's jaw to drop, or Strepticon to gasp in disbelief.

Beneath the advertisement was a photograph of Madame Vasari herself, complete with turban, bushy eyebrows and a beard like a rhododendron bush.

'Logios defend us,' Strepticon whispered. 'Isn't that ... Fentwick? He wouldn't!' He looked at Catterat wide eyed. 'Would he?'

Catterat snapped his jaw back into place. 'Inquiries will be made. In the meantime, let us establish what else we have to reckon with.'

Craning his neck to peer round Catterat's shoulder, Strepticon said, 'That notice at the corner's all right. They're the exam results I put up yesterday evening. The sooner the students get back to work the better. Particularly Findler. How a grown wizard can fail Theromancy Two five times is a mystery. An apprentice with half a brain could do the test underwater, with both hands tied behind his back, standing on his head!'

'Really?' An emotion stirred on the upper slopes of Catterat's face. For a moment he wasn't sure what it was. Many, many years had passed since he had found anything remotely funny. And this was more than funny: it was hilarious. He had to fight the urge to laugh out loud!

'According to this,' he tapped the results sheet, 'Findler has done rather well. In fact, the only failure this year appears to be . . .' He gave a faint smile. 'See for yourself.'

Strepticon looked, and saw, and gave a cry of rage and horror.

The name at which Catterat's finger pointed was Strepticon!

'But I passed with distinction forty years ago. You know I did.' He looked around wildly. 'Everyone knows! Ask Bloxifil!'

'I hardly think an anteater's testimony will be acceptable to the council, but if you wish me to make inquiries . . .'

'Ask anyone! How could I become a senior wizard if I'd failed Theromancy Two? It's a lie – a horrible, wicked lie.'

'Then it will be exposed as a lie as soon as the council completes its investigation. Until then, I'm afraid I shall have to suspend you.' He raised his hand to silence a cry of protest. 'Don't worry. We'll hush it up. No one but your oldest, dearest friends need ever know.'

Strepticon didn't seem to find this comforting. He fairly bounced up and down. 'Why should anyone know? The list's a pack of lies. Why can't I tear it up?'

'Think,' urged Catterat sternly, 'think what would happen if everyone were to suppress facts whenever they felt like it; the result would be chaos! Chaos, confusion, and grave breaches of prescribed procedures. May Logios guard us from that fate. Do you understand me?'

Strepticon understood that Catterat was not going to let the matter drop. He transferred his gaze sulkily to the adjoining notice, and pretended to find it fascinating. All of a sudden, he didn't need to pretend.

'In that case,' he said in a strange voice, 'the council had better be told of this too!'

Refectory Menu, week beginning 49th Rabilhar

Monday: Dragon's fin soup and vampire dumplings

Tuesday: Strained toad-broth with essence of lizard

Wednesday:	Pickled mice in a nest of winter greens
Thursday:	Beetroot fritter in fresh frogspawn
Friday:	Boiled roots with grated lungwort
Saturday:	Thistle jelly and bananas in oregano
Sunday:	Cold pigeons' feet

Tormenting Strepticon had almost made Catterat forget about being frightened, but the menu brought it all back again. The dishes looked mysteriously familiar – as if he knew what they were without being told. His stomach performed something along the lines of a small somersault, but despite this he managed to produce a creditable sniff. 'Perfectly straightforward. A sound, well-balanced menu, packed with nourishment. I fail to see why the council should be concerned.'

'Read the small print. Of course, if it doesn't bother *you* . . .'

Catterat didn't like the sound of this. When his stomach had executed a second unofficial somersault, he ran his eye down the menu, and located the line of small print at the bottom:

By Order of CORNELIUS CATTERAT, Chief Cook

A silence fell, so deep and treacherous it could have

swallowed a man like quicksand. When at last Catterat broke it, there was a pinched look round his mouth, but his voice was steady. 'You were right. Destroy the notices. Tear up every single one and burn the pieces. We never saw them. They never existed. We will not speak of them again.'

If Strepticon hoped for time to savour his triumph, he was to be disappointed. Shock had jolted Catterat's brain back to life. It was racing now, so fast he could hardly keep up.

How could he – how could anyone – feel safe in a universe where libellous announcements pinned themselves up over night? Where books could rewrite themselves while your back was turned? Where you might be Chief Wizard one minute, and a cook the next? Where even a man's own thoughts rebelled against him?

I KNEW it was oregano.

Catterat snatched the hat from his head and ground it under one foot. It made him feel better, but didn't address the basic question.

He must act, and act fast.

'When you've burned the pieces, call a meeting of the Council!' The Chief Wizard swept into the corridor and headed for the stairs at a gallop. 'We are going to take control!'

Chapter Eleven

'Hear ye, hear ye!'

The cry rang in Kevin's ears just long enough to wake him, before it was drowned by clanging. He sat up in alarm. Had he slept so long that Yurt had arrived already? But why would he turn up shouting and clanging a bell?

'Under its emergency powers, the Wizards' Council does this forty-ninth day of Rabilhar call upon and command all citizens of Stolk –'

Clang! 'That means you.'

'– to surrender to its appointed representatives—'

Clang! 'That's us.'

'– the following items.'

CLANG!

That didn't sound like Yurt. Kevin's heartbeat returned to normal. Draping the sheet around his shoulders, he went to see what was up.

Below, on the pavement opposite his window, stood a lanky red-haired youth in a brown long-tailed coat and very short purple trousers, armed with a bell. His companions were a fat, balding man swathed in a crumpled star-spangled cloak, and a tall, shabby individual sporting baggy cricket trousers and odd rugby socks.

By now Kevin had been in Theromantia long enough to guess he was looking at a trio of wizards. Who else would have the nerve to go out in broad daylight dressed like that?

'All books, pamphlets, newspapers, magazines and comics,' chanted the star-spangled cloak.

The youth clanged the bell and gave a reedy wail, 'Give them up!'

'All maps and charts pertaining to any territory whatsoever,' yelled the rugby socks.

More bell-ringing. 'Hand them over!' screeched the youth.

'All posters, notices, advertisements and captioned illustrations.'

Clang! 'Or else!'

'All letters, contracts, statements, accounts and handwritten material of any description.'

Clang! 'No matter what! It is Council's command.'

The chanting continued for several minutes more, but Kevin had stopped listening.

Contracts! he thought, with a great leap of the heart.

People were going to have to hand in all written matter, including contracts, to the Wizards' Council! If Yurt complied – and people did seem to be complying: already the pile of books and papers was big enough to block the pavement – Kevin was off the hook.

It was not until he had pulled on his socks that he thought what else people were being told to hand in.

Such as books, for instance.

The last time he'd held a book was at Alison's up in Similon's attic. That was only five days ago, although it seemed more like years. In those days, he thought nostalgically, he'd still been one hundred per cent himself: Kevin Young, future chartered accountant, who couldn't pick a lock or cheat an alligator-wrestler if he tried. The last time he'd looked at a map was back in the same golden age, peering over Alison's shoulder at Similon's circle.

Without being able to say precisely why, the idea of handing over to the council either that map or the volume of Logios containing Theorem 39 made Kevin suddenly uneasy.

The two older wizards were hammering on doors. Soon the pile of articles beside the bell-ringer had grown to a mountain. What on earth was the council going to do with the stuff? Was there a storeroom somewhere – in the castle, perhaps – vast enough to hold it all?

CLANG! 'Bring out your books, your magazines, your comics,' shrilled the youth one last time. 'Bring out your books to be burned!'

'Gran!' Kevin shouted in horror, flailing with both fists against the door. 'Let me out! There's something I've got to do!'

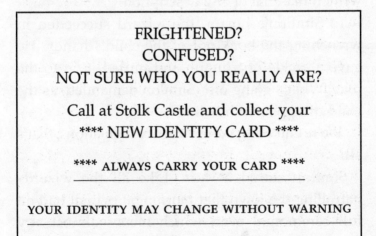

FRIGHTENED?
CONFUSED?
NOT SURE WHO YOU REALLY ARE?

Call at Stolk Castle and collect your
**** NEW IDENTITY CARD ****

**** ALWAYS CARRY YOUR CARD ****

YOUR IDENTITY MAY CHANGE WITHOUT WARNING

Similon was not so much reading this notice, taped to the foot of the statue, as staring through it, when a hand reached past him and ripped it down.

'You! Septic!' said a brusque voice. 'Got any writing on you?'

Flinching at the sound of a nickname he'd always hated, Similon turned reluctantly and recognised Epzimot, a wizard several years his junior. Beyond, two other wizards, whose faces were vaguely familiar, were supervising the construction of a gigantic bonfire at the far side of the square. He blinked, bewildered, as he caught sight of a fourth wizard who seemed to be fighting a small girl for possession of a picture book. 'What?'

'Have you concealed upon your person any books, magazines, leaflets, pamphlets or other written material of any description?'

To Similon's horror, the wizard succeeded in wrenching the book out of the child's hands. He gave a cackle of triumph and hurled it on to the pile. 'What's going on?' Similon demanded, as the child disappeared howling.

'We're enforcing the emergency regulations, that's all.'

Similon stared at him. Like all the wizards patrolling the town that morning, Epzimot had on full ceremonial gear, which means almost any combination of garments that would never, in any circumstances, be worn by a normal person. In his case, full dress was a livid tartan dinner jacket, a tennis pullover, red braces and a pair of grubby tennis shorts. His knees were blue with cold, and the unwizardly thought flashed into Similon's mind that he looked ridiculous.

'Does it look as if I'm carrying any books?' he asked with a flicker of spirit.

'How you look isn't relevant. Are you or aren't you? Yes or no?'

The flicker died. Arguing wouldn't make life any better. Nothing was going to make his life better ever again. Similon sighed. 'No.'

'Keep it that way, Septic.' Epzimot wagged an officious finger. 'Even wizards aren't allowed books now, let alone common criminals like you.'

To his own surprise, Similon hardly minded the insult. It was quite right to call him a criminal. If he hadn't wanted to disprove Theorem 39, none of this would be happening.

Epzimot loped over to the side of the square and, with one swift gesture, wrenched a sign off a wall. Before the thin metal crumpled beneath the wizard's boot, Similon glimpsed what it said: BAXTENBRAT SQUARE.

Yes, he was a criminal.

'Rip down the street names!' Epzimot's voice had grown hoarse from shouting, a raucous whisper that made Similon shiver. 'Smash the statues! Hand over your trophies, your coin collections, your medals!

145

Turn in your certificates, your photographs, your stamp albums. Don't try to hide them! The crystal ball sees everything. Bring them all out or we'll come in and get them! Throw them all on to the fire!'

With each cry, Epzimot bowled an item high on to the top of the heap. In the meantime, Trebiwill fumbled among the loose papers at the edge. A photograph began to smoulder. Almost at once, a tongue of flame shot into the air, and then another. Within seconds, the whole mountain was ablaze.

Turning in the other direction, he saw thick clouds of smoke spreading above the rooftops from half a dozen different sources. They must be lighting fires all over town.

Never in the history of Theromantia had wizards done such a thing. Similon thought he knew whose fault it was that wizards were doing it now.

His. It had to be. He hung his head in shame.

In the gutter by his right foot lay a half-eaten apple core. Remembering Zlot, he picked it up and dropped it in his pocket, taking care to keep his fingers out of biting range. A hamster couldn't live in a pocket for ever, but he couldn't turn it out to starve or get trampled in what was rapidly becoming a riot.

The thought floated into his head that he could take Zlot home and set him free.

Home.

A lump rose in Similon's throat. Closing his eyes, he found himself yearning passionately not for his books or the tools of his trade, but for the dog-eared postcard of Venice that he'd pinned up next to his bed after it came through the letterbox by mistake, the dinosaur's thighbone he used to prop the window open on stuffy evenings, and the strange rock he'd found in the recreation ground, which looked like a duck. More than anything else in the world, he longed to go home.

But he couldn't. Not yet.

He rose clumsily to his feet and tried to dust off his trousers. Epzimot was right to call him a criminal, but he wasn't the kind of criminal who walks away from what he's done. He wasn't a wizard any more, but he could still try to put things right.

And with a terrible sinking feeling, he knew where he had to begin.

The Organisation had its own methods of responding to a raid. Crouched in the recess behind a kitchen cupboard, hugging a stack of books and papers, Alison found these methods extremely uncomfortable. She couldn't straighten up for fear of being spotted by one of the wizards who was searching the house. She couldn't even shift her feet, because the cat, for reasons best known to itself, had chosen to share her hiding-place. There was a very real danger that if she moved a fraction, she'd tread on it.

She was worried about Fentwick too.

He claimed to understand how reality regrowth worked. If anyone could take a change of identity in his stride, it should have been him. Instead of which, he'd gone right out of control.

'Frog off,' he'd snarled at the fourth visitor of the morning to come knocking for Madame Vasari. When the man showed signs of arguing, he added, 'Or I can personally guarantee that the only future you'll have is as a snail. Got that? Good!'

'You're hopeless,' Mave said as she watched the man trail away. 'Ten ducats you could have earned. All you had to do was tell his fortune. We could do with the money.'

'I'm a wizard, not a newting fortune-teller. If the council finds out about this nonsense, I'll get struck off.'

'Why?' Alison demanded.

'Because fortune-telling is lies, that's why! Nobody can foretell the future.'

There was something wrong there, although for a while she hadn't been able to spot what it was. She went on listening with half an ear as the argument spluttered on.

'I suppose wizards never tell lies then?'

'Only in pursuit of a higher truth!'

'Only when it suits them, you mean.'

'Poppycock!' By this time Fentwick was so livid that Alison wouldn't have been surprised to see smoke come out of his ears. 'Don't meddle with ideas that don't concern you.'

Suddenly Alison saw where his line of reasoning fell down. 'Wait a minute!' she cried. 'What about reality regrowth?'

'What?'

Mave and Fentwick seemed equally reluctant to break off their dispute. Raising her voice, Alison went on, 'Nobody can foretell the future.' She looked at Fentwick. 'That's what you just said.'

'Of course it's what—'

'And what I said was, what about reality regrowth? If reality regrowth changes everything, why shouldn't it change that too?'

Fentwick opened his mouth and then closed it again. Mave looked at him, and then at Alison. 'You mean Madame Vasari might actually be able to tell people's fortunes?' she asked incredulously. 'Really and truly? No making it up? And Madame Vasari's him?'

Alison nodded. She was watching Fentwick closely. Beneath the dense facial shrubbery she saw a jumble of emotions – fear, outrage, and disbelief – fly across his face.

Good, she thought at the time. High time he found out what it was like being told you're someone else.

Later, however, she was less sure.

Already teetering on the brink of an explosion, he stumped off to the office. There he opened Sep's volume of Logios, and discovered it had been reality-adjusted overnight.

Ye Compleet Wyrkes of Aelfrede Baxtenbrat included a Theorem 39, but it had nothing to do with barriers. It dealt with an enchantment called temporal translocation, which Fentwick said was something no decent wizard would be caught dead lizarding about with. They had left him skimming the contents of the book frantically, page by page, in the hope of stumbling on something halfway relevant. Looking in later to see how he was getting on, they found him using the book as a football.

'Pompous, worm-infested, frog-ridden bore! Man was an imbecile. Never used one word if he could use a hundred. Couldn't write his way out of a wet paper bag! And this . . . this . . . caterpillar dropping is the wizard we have to kowtow to now, is it?' He gave a hair-raising growl and ripped out a handful of pages. 'Well, I newting well WON'T!'

He flung the torn-out pages into the air. As he seized a second handful, Alison shrieked, 'Don't! That's Sep's book, not yours!'

'Go on!' cried Mave, dancing with glee. 'Let him! All their silly books are rubbish. Down with the wizards!'

It was at this moment that the hammering on the front door started. Alison scooped up as many pages of Baxtenbrat as she could before scuttling into her hiding-place, and it was a good thing she did. Far from trying to save Sep's book, Fentwick greeted the wizard patrol like long-lost brothers and asked to chuck *Ye Compleet Wyrkes* on the fire himself.

Despite the best intentions, a tear welled up over Alison's lower eyelid and trickled down one cheek. How could someone as intelligent as that be so stupid?

Sep had used the book to create his barrier, and in her eyes that meant it mattered – at the very least because, as long as it existed, there was a chance reality would relent and adjust it back into something useful. How could that happen once it was reduced to a handful of ashes?

The front door slammed. Mave's light footsteps pattered up the hall. 'They've gone. You can come out.'

No Fentwick, then. Alison found she wasn't surprised. He was probably out in the street with his friends, dancing round the fire.

As she began to wriggle out of her hiding place,

151

her arms round Mave's books, she remembered her own. At that very moment, some horrible wizard was probably at 38 Field End Road ripping them off the shelves – her shelves, which she'd put up herself when she'd hauled her box of books down from the attic the week before Sep came.

Wizards were all the same, she thought, blinking furiously. Doing just what they wanted without giving a fig for anyone else. Anyone would think Logios had given them the right to make up the rules as they went along! Mave had the right idea; they weren't to be trusted – not even ones like Sep, who seemed harmless. For crying out loud, it was Sep who'd started it!

Down with the wizards! whispered a voice inside Alison's head. For once she didn't care less if it was her own or Zelda's.

'Down with the wizards!' she said fiercely as Mave came into the kitchen. 'It's time for Plan X!'

The mountains were to his right.

Kevin knew this not because he could see them – the smoke was so thick that he hadn't been able to see much beyond his nose for the past ten minutes – but because of what he had just bumped into. In the old days, when the A519 went somewhere, he'd sometimes taken the 72 bus along it from Axborough to Eastgate. The bus was always late, and as a result he was something of an expert on the shape of the broken bench at the bus stop and the pattern of the metal rubbish bin.

Right, he thought, concentrating. If the mountains were over there, Field End Road couldn't be more than a ten-minute walk away. He had to cross the road, go on a bit, and take the first left. After that he could sort of feel his way as he went along. Even if the street names had been reality-adjusted, or ripped down by the wizards, he though he'd recognise Alison's house when he saw it. And it ought still to be number thirty-eight, provided reality hadn't started playing with numbers as well as words.

On top of that, Alison's house was the dead centre of Similon's circle. He had a hunch he'd somehow *know* when he got there. There'd be a sign of some kind – a sign you couldn't miss, even in a murk like peasoup, in a reality-adjusted landscape.

'Right,' he said firmly to the litter bin, 'this is going to be easy.' He said it three times before it sounded convincing.

A quarter of an hour later, he revised his theory. It wasn't going to be easy, and the only reason he wasn't heading straight back to his gran's was that he hadn't a clue how to get there.

Or anywhere else.

The first turning on the left ended in a clump of

firs so thick he couldn't squeeze between them. The next turning he found – and he couldn't tell how many paths the trees and rocks had swallowed in between – was, if anything, worse. The thick, still air was filled with furtive noises: creaks, pops, and heavy, breathy bubbling. No animal was responsible for them, because there were none. Kevin's impression was that the sounds came from the ground itself.

He tiptoed on, trying to walk without putting his feet down, and wondering how the boulders that littered the street had got there.

Plop . . .

He spun round and fell over a knee-high boulder specked with lichen that had sprung up from nowhere right behind him. Sprawled across it as he was, he felt the exact second at which it began to quiver, but before he could scramble off, it gave another *plop*, and his feet left the ground. Just behind it, a patch of tarmac bulged upwards and then split as another boulder nudged its way to the surface. And then another . . .

Mr Davis, who taught football at Westbury High, would have been stunned to witness the turn of speed his worst athlete managed over very difficult terrain. All that halted Kevin's headlong flight was the sight of a line of red traffic cones stretched across his path. A string of orange lamps swung between them, winking in the gloom. By their light he read the sign that was propped against one cone:

DANGER!
REALITY REGROWTH IN PROGRESS!
YOU ARE ADVISED TO
TURN BACK!

Kevin looked back, and gulped. He couldn't turn back.

'Let's talk about this,' he heard himself whisper.

He groaned. If the voice of Grork was back, it was a sign he was in real trouble.

He flung himself sideways in the nick of time as a geyser the height of a skyscraper exploded beside his left foot. Reality was in no mood to negotiate.

All right. He couldn't go back, and it was suicide to stay where he was. There was only one thing he could do . . .

When he reached 38 Field End Road, what felt like a lifetime later, he almost missed it.

Through the dense smoke the house looked no different from the others he'd passed at a gallop. He stopped outside not because instinct told him he'd arrived, but because he had a stitch and he had to stop somewhere. He had sagged against the gate, wiping his streaming eyes on the sleeve of his coat, when he felt an indefinable change in the atmosphere.

He lifted his head and tried without knowing why to peer upwards. That was when it happened again – not a noise, a vibration, a silent rearrangement of the air as a huge body stretched itself.

That's funny, he thought as the gloom above shifted. The roof's moving. He was surprised roofs did that, even in Theromantia. Not as surprised as he would have been a week earlier, of course.

And nothing like as surprised as he was ten seconds later. As the roof lifted itself off the house, unfurled its wings and flapped away into the darkness, Kevin fainted.

Crouched among the rubble, Fentwick told himself that what had happened was perfectly logical. And if it was logical, it ought to have been predicted. So why had no one – including Madame Vasari – predicted it?

Light a fire, and what do you get?

Smoke.

Light twenty fires, and what you get is lots of smoke, billowing up over the spires and chimneys, darkening the sun. Within an hour, the sky is black. Day turns to night. And then what?

He lifted his head and peered round the remains

of a wall. Here and there, fires smouldered on, but the pall of smoke had lifted. It was early afternoon, he calculated – two o'clock at the latest. It should stay light for another couple of hours, and while it was light it was safe to move. Before night fell in earnest, he meant to have something a great deal more solid than bricks or tiles between him and Similon's most terrible creation. There was only one place he could think of worth trying.

He stood up and began to thread his way through the debris.

When day becomes night, what happens is this: night's creatures awaken. Hamsters nibble, owls swoop, badgers shuffle, bats glide ... but these aren't the problem. The problem is the thelamungus, who wakes hungry as always, whose wings blot out the last rays of light as it takes to the air.

The wizards had made a poor showing, himself included. One glimpse of those terrible beaks and they had run like rabbits, albeit elderly, unathletic ones. Of course, that hadn't saved them. And of course, when they had nowhere else to run, when they could feel the beaks snapping at their tired heels, despite Catterat's warnings and Bloxifil's example, they had tried magic – not the new, incomprehensible Baxtenbrat variety, but the old, familiar Logios kind. If he hadn't found a hole to crawl into in the nick of time, Fentwick thought he'd have done the same himself.

Something stirred behind a pile of bricks. A clumsy shape emerged into the open. It saw Fentwick, and shuffled up to him, whining.

Fentwick looked down at the spiny anteater.

'Shalazar, old chap?' He gave it a tentative pat on the shoulder.

'Come along with me. I'm going to make for the one place the thelamungus will never break into; the castle. We'll see who we can pick up on the way.'

Chapter Twelve

The map was by the window, under the splinters of Sep's desk. This was a stroke of luck: if it had been on the desk it would have been covered in bird mess, like everything else.

Kevin had once heard a biology teacher say you could learn a lot about a creature by studying the place where it lived. All Kevin was willing to bet was that this creature had an upset stomach. Not surprising, really – he stooped to remove a spike from the sole of his boot – in view of the fact that it seemed to have been eating querulite balls and hedgehogs.

Fentwick! The sight of the ball embedded in a mound of bird mess brought the professor vividly to mind. Kevin had a horrible vision of thelamungus swooping down on the wizard unawares while he waited in the attic. If so, his last remains were probably spattered all around, unrecognisable among the general filth.

He blinked hard, and set to work using the spike to dig out the globe of querulite. After that he scraped the ball as clean as he could, squeezed it into his pocket, and stood up. There was no point searching the attic for the right volume of Logios, or for any other book. He was no naturalist, but he could see that the thelamungus liked paper, and what it liked to do with it was shred it, chew it, and smear the resulting paste all over its nest. In a matter of days, it had built up a disgusting layer all round the attic walls.

The wizards wouldn't need to confiscate the contents of Sep's library; the thelamungus had beaten them to it.

But he had the map and ball, at any rate. Now, if he could only find Zelda—

He shook his head sharply. Ever since he'd opened his eyes to see a lattice of twigs above his nose, and discovered he was lying on his back with his head in a hedge, he'd felt distinctly peculiar.

All he had to do was find *Alison*. Together they

could work out how to track down Sep—

Great. Zelda will know what to do. Wonder if she's still wearing that black outfit?

Kevin shook his head again. It didn't matter what she was wearing. The point was to find her, find Sep, and then—

Sell him the map! Brilliant!

What?

Must be worth a few ducats, a historic document like that. Hey, I could have an auction!

'No auction. I *give* Sep the map.' Kevin wished his head didn't feel as if it was full of bubbles. 'It's his map we're talking about. I can't start selling someone his own property.'

Grorks can. It's a family tradition.

Kevin realised that his head wasn't the only part that hurt: his legs were like lead, blood was oozing through a tear in the right knee of his trousers, and he had skinned the palms of both hands. He wanted to lie down somewhere warm and peaceful, and have his wounds dabbed with cotton wool and antiseptic.

Feeling dizzier by the second, he would have curled up on the floor where he was except for the obvious risk of blood-poisoning.

Zelda'll know what to do. Ask Zelda.

He tucked the map into his coat and limped towards the stairs. Keep your mind on what you have to do, he told himself sternly. You've found the map; now all you have to do is find . . . find . . .

He slipped on the third stair and went down the rest of the flight on the seat of his trousers. As he picked himself up, the house rocked.

That would be the thelamungus arriving home. Kevin propped himself up against the wall and waited to faint again. When nothing happened, he began to wonder if he was past panicking – if he had somehow gone right through fear and come out the other side? That seemed the only possible explanation; after everything that had happened, he was simply too frightened to be frightened any more.

He stood up, muzzily pleased to have worked that out.

Immunity to panic might not last indefinitely, though. Even vaccinations didn't last for ever. Better get a move on and . . . what was it he had to do again? Ah, that was it!

Kevin thanked his lucky stars he'd had the sense to leave the creaky front door open. He tiptoed down the last flight of stairs and slipped out into the garden.

That was what he had to do, of course: find Zelda.

It ought to have been part of Theromancy Two, Similon thought miserably.

Question: How does a wizard with a poor sense of direction and a bad blister climb a wolf-infested mountain in thick smoke?

Answer: If he has any sense, he doesn't. Because if he tries, when the smoke clears he'll find himself crouching on top of a spiky bush, counting wolves.

There were seventeen, or maybe eighteen. If only they would keep still for a minute, he'd be certain. It was all the circling and weaving that made it hard to keep track.

One part of him was still rational enough to know that it didn't make much difference whether he was torn apart by seventeen wolves or eighteen. The other part of him was still one hundred per cent wizard, with a passion for useless information. That part pushed common sense aside and went on counting.

The castle walls loomed up against the grey sky. The next time he lost count, he cast a longing glance upwards. Inside those solid walls – at least as thick as the length of a wizard's staff at the point where they rose from the rock – lay something that mattered almost as much to him as his own skin: the hint of a way to unlock the barrier.

He shivered, wondering whether, if he had reached the castle, he would have had the nerve to put his theory to the test. He hoped so, but it looked as if he'd never find out.

He sighed and went back to counting.

Twenty-three, he groaned a minute later. Was every frogging wolf on the mountain rolling up to join in the fun?

They were getting friskier, he couldn't help noticing. His heart had already sunk further than he would have thought anatomically possible, and now it was down somewhere in the vicinity of his left big toe. Any minute now the brutes would realise that he was well within leaping distance. And then . . .

Something brushed his neck. He flinched instinctively, and then flinched again as he saw the hamster clinging to his collar. 'What do you want?' he asked, uneasy.

It let out an incomprehensible stream of squeaks, like the ones that had greeted the apple core.

'For the love of Logios,' Similon said wearily, 'how do you expect me to understand if you won't talk Universal? Try again, slowly.'

The hamster hopped up and down, squeaking, then sprang up and sank its teeth in the lobe of Similon's left ear.

It was the last thing the wizard was expecting. He gave a cry of anguish, leaped out of the thorn-bush, and landed heavily on a large wolf. While this was still in a state of shock, he picked himself up and streaked up the path to the castle, scattering wolves in every direction.

'Let me in!' he shrieked, pounding the massive gates with frantic fists. 'I'm in mortal danger. Sanctuary! Araaggh!'

The last cry was one of surprise as the doors swung inwards and he found himself careering across the entrance hall at something between a stagger and a gallop. Hopelessly off balance, he stumbled on unchecked until he tripped over a large, long-nosed animal.

'Araaggh!' he said unoriginally, and fell on the flagstones.

'Similon!' said a familiar voice. 'I knew it was going to be you, frog it. I was having a nap in the chair there, and suddenly I dreamed you – right down to the hamster. Now you're here you'd better leave that anteater alone, remove the hamster from your ear, and start talking.'

It was Fentwick. Similon stared up at him, too dazed to obey orders. 'It's not just a hamster, it's Zlot. The brute bites, and he won't talk Universal. I'm at my wits' end, I don't mind telling you. And the wolves!' He cowered as Fentwick, with a bark of impatience, advanced upon him. 'Please don't do anything nasty – I couldn't bear it. Oh! Thanks!'

Holding the hamster by the tail at arm's length, Fentwick strode over to the ceremonial suit of armour which stood at the foot of the stairs. He slid the visor down and dropped the hamster inside. A

stream of furious squeaks floated out to them through the gap under the visor.

'He doesn't like that,' Similon said, sitting up. 'And he won't have anything to eat. I don't want him to starve.'

'Then drop him food through the visor. For the love of Logios, stop being difficult! Thanks to you, I – with my hitherto unblemished record – will now figure in histories as the supervisor whose pupil left the better part of Stolk a smoking ruin, and saw to it that there were more anteaters than wizards in Theromantia! And that's not all: if word gets out about this Madame Vasari nonsense, I'll be lucky if I escape charges. All in all, you'll understand my asking what exactly you plan to do about it, you newtbrained nincompoop?'

Similon swallowed hard, and told him.

In a crisis, what is a wizard's first instinct?

To call a meeting.

As a rule, the graver the crisis, the longer the meeting. In all the annals of Theromantia, no council had ever faced such a desperate situation as the one Catterat convened in Westleigh High staffroom that fateful afternoon, yet no council ever completed its business faster.

Of the seventeen wizards who had set out to purge Stolk of written matter, only one had returned, bearing dreadful tidings and reeking of wood-smoke. He trembled as he stammered out his report, plucking at the charred tatters of his ceremonial clothes as he spoke. His seven listeners trembled too as they heard him.

How long till nightfall, when the same fate lay in store for them?

A fog had rolled in. From the staffroom window Catterat found it hard to make out the line of foam where the waves broke on the roof of the science block. The wind screamed and the pane of glass shook beneath his fingers. A storm was coming to cut the short day even shorter. Minutes, not hours, of daylight were were all that remained. And he knew as well as any wizard that only one place offered protection against the thelamungus.

'We should never have left the castle!'

The Chief Wizard turned in order to direct a bleak stare at the speaker. Grunvelt, the council's specialist on equilibration, glared back. His defiant eyes had the short-sighted stare of a bad-tempered mole.

'If we had stayed, we would have starved,' someone argued.

Grunvelt snorted. For that snort alone, the Chief Wizard was tempted to strike him, but worse was to come. 'I'd rather starve than eat another breakfast like the one this morning. What in the name of Logios was it supposed to be, eh?' He glanced at

Strepticon, his usual ally in disputes, but the Treasurer seemed absorbed in a minute adjustment to one sleeve of his gown. Grunvelt gave another snort, louder.

'Toad vomit?' he suggested with a horrible attempt at playfulness. 'Frizzled sea snake? Logios preserve me from another such concoction!'

'That can be arranged,' said Catterat, deadly calm. 'As to the castle, it hardly requires a first-class degree in equilibration to see that in the current crisis, it offers the best protection. I take it that everyone present agrees we should return forthwith?'

Even for the sake of argument – a cause dear to the heart of the entire council – nobody was prepared to vote against the motion.

'Good.' His expression thawing by a couple of degrees, Catterat went on. 'In that case, I call upon Bloxifil to report on the current carpet situation. For the sake of those of you whose knowledge of Universal is a little rusty, I will translate.'

The anteater lumbered to the centre of the circle, where it uttered a series of snorts, then turned its snout expectantly towards Catterat.

'Some of us brought carpets with us, but these are single-seater models, not built for use in reality reflux. Since time is short and we cannot reach our goal on foot, the only alternative seems to be a carpet adaptation. He has therefore attached a modified control panel to a—' Catterat hesitated and looked enquiringly across at the anteater, then continued evenly, 'to an eight-seater plastic tablecloth. He estimates that there is no higher than a one-in-three chance that this will fail to operate in a satisfactory fashion.'

The anteater grunted urgently.

'Theoretically speaking.'

The silence with which the council received this information was a thoughtful one. Yet one by one, they raised a hand, or paw, to indicate consent. What alternative had they?

When the vote was over, Strepticon, at a nod from Catterat, strode to the staffroom door and flung it open. 'Apprentices!' he wailed shrilly. 'Attend for your orders!'

Charufex, the Apprentice Master, cleared his throat in an embarrassed fashion. 'There aren't any apprentices.' He wilted as everyone turned to look at him. 'There were a few left yesterday, but what with high tide last night and this morning's unpleasantness, we seem to have run out. It's irregular, I admit, but . . .' he flung his hands wide and shrugged. 'Special circumstances. I will, of course, get in a fresh supply as soon as possible.'

'Conscript the native youths,' Grunvelt growled. 'They can't be worse than the last batch, Logios knows.'

'There are no native youths left either. Not on the premises, anyway. People claimed them.' A note of wonder crept into Charufex's voice. 'They seemed genuinely glad to see the young brutes. It was really quite extraordinary.'

'Indeed?' Catterat made no attempt to conceal his impatience. 'The human heart is an unfathomable mystery. Now, if you would care to fetch the table-cloth from behind the sofa, I suggest we remove to a suitable take-off area without delay.'

Five minutes later, seven wizards and one over-weight anteater huddled together on top of a plastic tablecloth, at the edge of the sandy waste outside the assembly hall.

'Brace yourselves!' cried Catterat as the anteater lowered its snout. 'The first moments will be decisive. May Logios protect us all!'

Strepticon looked up. 'And Baxtenbrat,' he quavered. Everyone looked at him. Bloxifil lifted his snout from the controls. 'I mean, I know he was wrong, but in the circumstances, don't you think . . . ? To be on the safe side?'

'I will try to forget you said that,' said Catterat icily. 'We are wizards, followers of Logios. If we go to a glorious death, so be it. I will neither live nor die a disciple of Baxtenbrat. Enough!' He signalled to Bloxifil. 'We will go!'

Strepticon, to whom the notion of a glorious death

had little appeal, let out a wail. 'I've changed my mind. I want to get off . . . f . . . f' The cry was sucked into the fog as the carpet shot into space.

'Baxtenbrat protect us,' whispered an echo from the clouds. Then there was only the sand, the booming sea, and silence.

Passing through the digestive system of a large carnivore hadn't damaged the ball in any obvious sense. On the other hand, it hadn't made it any easier to operate. After what felt like hours, all Kevin had succeeded in seeing was a horrible fish-like monster marked with a large black dot. He'd peered at it for ages before realising it was his own eye.

He tried again to cast his mind back to the night when he'd seen Fentwick use the ball. He thought the wizard had controlled it via an area that worked like a viewfinder. The obvious candidate was a chipped rectangle that looked as if it was made of different material from the rest of the ball, but although Kevin tapped every spot on the surface of it, the ball stayed stubbornly blank. He'd have given up on it if he'd had a clue how else to find Zelda.

Maybe there was an <u>on/off</u> switch somewhere? Kevin peered at it in mounting frustration, aware that even a fraction of what he didn't know about querulite balls would fill a large book. Trust the school to leave important topics like that off the curriculum. When was the last time a teacher had mentioned querulite in a chemistry lesson, or demonstrated how to operate a simple crystal ball, he asked himself bitterly? Never!

Suddenly dizzy, he closed his eyes and leaned back against the bus-stop. The only thing to do was to try to visualise every tiny detail of what Fentwick had done and said that night.

Well, for a start, he had practically snatched the ball out of Kevin's hands. Could that be significant?

Feeling extremely silly, Kevin placed the ball in his right hand, counted to ten, and then snatched it away with his left.

The querulite didn't even flicker.

All right: what about a password?

Kevin racked his brains for magic words or phrases. 'Abracadabra!' he cried, without much hope. 'Open sesame! Gesundheit!'

No surprise this time that the ball stayed black as ink: he couldn't remember Fentwick saying anything the least like that when he snatched the ball. All the wizard had done was yell at him to hand it over: 'Come on, come on!' as if Kevin was some sort of halfwit. 'Come on come on come ON!'

Come on? Kevin's eyes flew open and he sat up straight. Come *on*? *Come ON*!

'Come ON, come ON!' The bellow would have done credit to a real wizard. 'You've *got* to work. Come on come on COME ON!'

And that was all it took.

Under his astonished eyes, the inky blackness lightened to pale grey, sprinkled with specks of snow. The ball was working!

The first image offered a nightmare glimpse of wolves, more wolves than he had ever seen or imagined, massed on a rocky ledge outside a fantastic castle. They faced the massive castle gates with an air that was at once forlorn and expectant. They reminded Kevin of dogs waiting for their master – only what sort of master kept dogs like those?

No answer: the castle vanished, and without a pause Kevin was in a gloomy corridor strung with cobwebs, watching Sep tiptoe through the shadows. Another figure walked ahead of him, unrolling a ball of string. He couldn't see who this was until the corridor branched, and they stopped to argue which way to go. Sep's companion cast a hunted look over his shoulder, and Kevin's heart flipped.

It was Fentwick, and he was scared witless.

No time for relief that he was alive; the vision fled, and Kevin was staring instead at a stormy sky, sliced through by flashes of lightning. Threading its way in and out of the clouds at high speed was a plastic tablecloth. It remained in view for a split second – enough for Kevin to see that the pilot was an anteater. In the circumstances, he thought it was doing a remarkable job.

Swish! The tablecloth screamed into a dive, and in that instant, with a start that almost made him drop the querulite, Kevin was face to face with Zelda.

She was in a dark place with rough-cut walls and a low, jagged ceiling. She was frowning – not at him, of course, at the girl who was with her. Scowling like that, she reminded him terribly of somebody, but he couldn't think who.

Alison? Was that who it was?

Someone called Alison . . .?

The spell of dizziness this time was so severe it left him feeling sick. He leaned against the bus stop. When the worst had passed, he opened his eyes again.

It didn't matter who Zelda looked like. The point was to focus on her long enough to find out where she was, so that he could track her down, and give her the . . .

Kevin blinked. He was sure he was meant to give Zelda something – something important too – but he had no idea what. He must have taken one knock on the head too many. Better concentrate on finding her, and worry about why later. It was bound to come back to him.

He rolled the ball again, and saw Zelda reaching up for something that dangled from a hook at the side of the tunnel.

What was it? A key?

He peered even closer.

At that moment, as her fingers closed round the object, something went seriously wrong in his head. For no reason at all, so far as he could gather, sirens wailed, buzzers buzzed, and a flashing light exploded behind his eyeballs.

Kevin Young might need to peer into a ball; the voice of Grork didn't. A split second was enough.

No! The wail of panic from within Kevin's skull brought him leaping to his feet. *Don't! Zelda*!

Chapter Thirteen

Mave watched Alison zip the key into her pocket. Her trust would have been touching if it weren't so misplaced. The past twenty-four hours had made one thing clear as querulite: telling Mave she wasn't Zelda was a waste of breath. If there was a way to shake the doorkeeper's confidence, Alison hadn't found it.

Life would be a lot simpler if she were Zelda.

For one thing, she'd know what Plan X was, and why it involved – as Mave fervently assured her – lugging an incredibly heavy backpack through an underground tunnel that appeared to go on for ever. What in six dimensions was in the wretched bag anyway? And why was it vital not to open it until Plan X was successful?

'*You* know,' was all Mave would say. 'I'm not to talk about it. Ever. Not even to you, you said.'

Alison could see why someone in Zelda's position didn't go broadcasting her intentions to all and sundry, but her own task would have been a good deal easier if Mave's sister hadn't taken secrecy quite so far.

She sighed, and tried an indirect approach. 'Remind me what this key is for, Mave.'

The doorkeeper favoured her with a stare of owlish reproach. 'We both know *I* asked *you* that exact same question at the last committee meeting. You wouldn't tell me, or any of the others. You said the fewer people who knew, the better, because it was dangerous. Remember?'

If only she did. Was the key dangerous to know about, or only dangerous to use? Alison's inner voice seemed to have switched off. Reality adjustment, which had sat on so many pieces of vital information, wasn't giving an update on that either.

Well, she couldn't stay where she was for ever. Go on, or go back? When you came down to it, there wasn't a lot to go back to.

'Come on.' Alison picked up the backpack,

winced as the straps bit into the sore places on her shoulders, and headed doggedly down the tunnel.

Almost immediately it turned sharp left, and she found their way barred by a metal portcullis.

The surge of relief she felt surprised her. However, just as she was thinking that that settled things, and they'd have to go back, Mave gave a crow of satisfaction. 'That's what the key's for!'

Of course: in the middle of the portcullis was a wooden gate, and the ends of the chain that held it shut were fastened by a padlock.

'Well done, Mave,' Alison said with a sinking heart as she unzipped her pocket and extracted the key.

Rats. It fitted.

She slid the chain free and gingerly opened the door. Mave darted through without a sign of anxiety. Alison's sinking feeling returned with a vengeance as she followed, and heard the door thud shut behind her.

What on earth had made her imagine she could execute Plan X without knowing what it was? She must have lost her mind. Even if by some fluke she pulled it off, had she any reason to believe it really would topple the power of the wizards?

There was only one possible honest answer: No.

'Why have we stopped?' Mave demanded. 'Next

time, warn me, or give a hand signal, or something. I almost tripped over you.'

'Sorry. Just thinking.'

On the other hand, what alternative did she have? Even the tunnel beat cowering behind a kitchen cupboard until Fentwick sent a posse of wizards to drag her out.

At least down here she was doing something.

'Are we nearly there?' Mave asked behind her.

'Maybe.'

'I wish you'd say. This tunnel stinks.'

It did too, with a rank, almost animal odour which Alison had been trying not to dwell on. Her patience snapped. 'Look, if I could tell you, I would. I don't like this any more than you. We've got to put up with it, that's all. Remember why we're doing this: Down with the Wizards!'

'Down with the wizards!' echoed Mave in a subdued voice.

Since the portcullis, the tunnel had gone downhill in more ways than one. Rusty-coloured water dripped from the roof on to Alison's head, and lay in slimy puddles underfoot. The walls had a coating of furry scum – a form of algae, she guessed, lifting the lantern. It was like mouldy fur, brownish-orange in colour, although she could see a strange pale patch further along the tunnel on the right.

But when she went to peer at it, she found the

pale patch wasn't algae at all, but a faded notice:

KEEP OUT!
By order of
THE GRORKS

The Grorks? Any wish Alison had had to turn back suddenly evaporated. 'Who do they think they are?' she snapped, setting her jaw and splashing on down the passage without a moment's hesitation. 'It's not their tunnel!'

'It might be,' Mave pointed out as she splashed loyally after her.

'So what? No one's here to stop us. I'm fed up with being bossed about. First it's the wizards—'

'Down with the wizards!' Mave sang.

'— and next it's the Grorks! If you ask me, they're as bad as each other. We're going on. What can they do to us anyway?'

Dangling from a rusty loop of chain round the next bend in the tunnel was the answer. This took the form of a second notice, which read:

PRIVATE!
TRESPASSERS WILL BE EATEN

'Bluff!' Alison said, recovering pretty well in the

circumstances. 'Eaten? Please! Do they think we were born yesterday? Come on!'

She set off at a speed Mave found hard to match. 'Aren't the Grorks dangerous, though?' she puffed, when she had caught Alison up.

'Dangerous?'

'That's what you always told us. Especially the Grorkling.'

'What?'

'The last of the Grorks. Kevin the Terrible. No one knows who he is or where he's hiding. You said that made him the most dangerous of all.'

This wonderful description of Kevin provoked Alison to a yelp of mirth. This turned to one of dismay as she found herself ankle-deep in a puddle. Puddle? Looking down, she saw it was more like a river. Going on was going to mean not so much walking as wading.

'Oh, frogs,' she said in disgust, 'My feet are freezing. Look, if I said the Grorkling was dangerous, I was wrong. I know him personally, as it happens, and you can take my word for it that you've nothing to worry about. You ought to see him kick a football. The only person he's a danger to is himself!'

A body plummeted into their path through a round opening in the tunnel ceiling. It hit the rock floor like a sack of potatoes, uttered a cry, and staggered to its feet.

'Freeze!' croaked the voice of Grork. 'Nobody move a muscle.'

'Stop badgering me,' Similon said, exasperated. The past two hours had revealed a lot about Fentwick, including the fact that he couldn't tell his left from his right, and was scared of mice. The younger wizard had lost all awe where his supervisor was concerned. 'It's been twenty-five years. I said it would be difficult.'

'Difficult? It's newting well impossible! Why, for the love of Logios, didn't you make notes?'

'I'd been lost for days. I didn't think I was going to get out alive. Would you have made notes if you were me?'

Fentwick clutched at the shreds of his self-control and asked with unconvincing patience, 'Can you remember *anything* useful?'

'No!' Similon shouted. 'I was frightened. It was my first week here. I was looking for the library, but I put my ball of string down somewhere and I couldn't find it. Whichever way I went, there was nothing but corridors and staircases. You can see what this wing is like. I was at the end of my tether by the time I came to the storeroom.'

Fentwick counted to seventeen five times in Universal, before saying through gritted teeth,

'Right! Tell me everything you can remember about the storeroom.'

Similon thought hard. 'It was huge. I opened the door, and all I could see was shelf after shelf, in every direction, on and on, up and up. There was no end to them. And there was dust everywhere! I remember thinking it looked as if you could pick it up and roll it up like a blanket.'

Fentwick gave a grunt. After a moment's brooding he asked, 'Was there anything else on the shelves? Apart from . . . the items in question?'

Similon shook his head. 'I thought it was empty, like the other rooms. Then I spotted what looked like a bundle tucked against the wall on the far side. I was desperate by then, so I went to see what it was. And, of course, when I did, it was a complete waste of time so far as I could tell.' He shot an anxious glance at Fentwick, who was chewing his beard and muttering. 'It could still be a waste of time, you know. There was no name, or anything. Just the initials: A.B. It was the statue this morning that made me think of them. Without that, I wouldn't have given them another thought, let alone realised that—'

'That what you'd stumbled upon was the stuff of legend. Or, to put it another way, the longest-running joke in the history of Theromantia. You were unaware that you had found . . . that what you had actually found were—'

It was no good. To a wizard like Fentwick, steeped in the traditions of Logios, what he had to say was simply too shocking.

In the end it was Similon who swallowed hard and said in hoarse whisper, 'The boots of Baxtenbrat!'

'I don't *know* why you mustn't go on,' Kevin said for the umpteenth time. 'All I know is, you mustn't. This tunnel is terribly, terribly dangerous.'

'Everything's terribly, terribly dangerous,' Alison snapped, with some justification. 'How do you know this is worse?'

'I've got a feeling about it.' His brown eyes pleaded for understanding. In point of fact, feeling was far too weak a word for the firework display that erupted inside his skull every time she showed signs of setting off, but it was the best he could manage after his recent ordeal. This included an agonising sprint along the A519, squeezing through a manhole, wriggling on his stomach in the pitchdark for what seemed like for ever, and finally falling heavily though a porthole on to the rocky floor of the tunnel, all at the insistence of the voice of Grork, issuing instructions at fever pitch.

Then Mave had hit him on the head with a heavy backpack.

185

His audience weren't impressed. Mave snorted, and Alison said witheringly, 'You're always having feelings.'

'Not like this,' he said positively. 'This tunnel gives me a very bad feeling indeed, I give you my word of honour. Honest.'

The last two words were a mistake. As Mave pointed out, a Grork wouldn't recognise honesty or honour if they jumped up and bit him. 'Treachery, that's the Grork speciality. Well, you won't get a chance to betray us. You're our prisoner! Isn't he, Zelda? What shall we do with him?'

Alison came to a decision. 'We'll take him with us. That way he can't tell anyone where we're going—'

'I don't know where you're going. I keep trying to—'

'—and if there is danger ahead, he's our insurance policy.'

'Your what?' he asked with misgiving.

'Our insurance policy,' she repeated. 'This is Grork territory, right? If it wasn't, you wouldn't have known how to get here. And you're the Grorkling.' She beamed. 'Nothing bad's going to happen while we've got you with us. No one in Theromantia would dare lay a finger on the last of the Grorks.'

'They wouldn't?' Kevin ran his tongue over his

lips and said sincerely. 'I really hope you're right.'

'Where's the string?' Fentwick asked suddenly.

'I gave it to you.'

'You didn't,' said Fentwick quietly.

'All right, but I put it down beside you!' Suddenly the ducat dropped. Similon spun round aghast. 'You mean to say you've lost it?'

'Logios grant me patience,' said Fentwick with lethal softness. 'What I mean is *you've* lost it. And you know what that means?'

'We're lost?' volunteered Similon, with a provoking return of calm. 'We were almost out of string anyway. I very nearly mentioned it to you. But I didn't. I thought you might get worried.'

Fentwick waited with heavy patience until he had finished, then continued ruthlessly, 'What that means is, our only hope of getting out of here before next Thursday week is to find the boots of Baxtenbrat, and ask the maggot himself!'

Similon considered this statement at length before asking, 'Do you think he'll tell us?'

'He'll have no choice!' snarled Fentwick. 'That's the point, isn't it? He can't refuse the wearer of his own boots. Assuming that's what they are, and that they work.'

Similon was on the verge of pointing out that those were two pretty big assumptions when he heard a twittering noise in the distance.

No – not in the distance: a twittering noise that was growing louder by the second. To a Theromantian wizard, that meant just one thing. 'I say, Fentwick,' he said apprehensively. 'Do you hear that? It sounds an awful lot like bats. Long-eared vampire bats, to be precise. And if that's what they are—'

'They'll newting well eat us!' bellowed Fentwick. 'Run, I tell you. RUN!'

Chapter Fourteen

'If you'd made a proper job of being a Grork,' Alison said, as she groped for the next rung of the ladder, 'you wouldn't have let this happen.'

'It's not my fault!' his voice floated up the shaft, sounding aggrieved. 'I did my best to stop you, but you wouldn't listen. I said I was no good with alligators.' Kevin had just lost a shoe to a reptile twice his weight and felt he had a right to some sympathy. 'And if you're the most wanted outlaw in Theromantia—'

'She's the most wanted outlaw in the dimension,

as a matter of fact,' said Mave, from just above his head. 'Check your facts, Grorkling.'

Kevin gritted his teeth. 'My name is Grork – I mean, Young. And what I'm saying is, a top-notch criminal like Zelda ought to deal with alligators herself. Instead of legging it up the nearest ladder, without so much as saying where she was off to.'

'I didn't think you needed to be told,' Alison said meanly.

Mave took up the attack. 'And they were your alligators, guarding your treasure chests.' She stopped to puff, in a way that suggested to Kevin she was finding the climb hard work.

He sympathised; he was finding it hard work too. Either he was back to being himself again or the last of the Grorks also lacked athletic ability. He was slightly comforted by this thought. If someone was going to borrow his brain cells, it was nice to feel they had something in common.

'People shouldn't keep dangerous animals if they can't control them,' Mave went on, having caught her breath.

In his annoyance, he forgot he had no shoe, and stamped his foot painfully on the ladder. 'Ow! I've told you a hundred times, those alligators had nothing to do with me. They probably belong to Yurt. I think he hires them out to my gran – the other

Kevin's gran, I mean. I've been wondering where he kept them.' A disturbing possibility struck Kevin. 'They can't climb ladders, can they?' he asked anxiously.

'Of course not!' Alison spoke scornfully, but just the same all three climbers speeded up – so much so that they were forced to clamber on in silence.

The moment Alison lifted the trapdoor, she could feel the musty emptiness all around her. She held up the lantern. All she could see was a dusty waste. It was quiet, so quiet that the silence felt solid. The stillness pressed against her, waiting to swallow her up.

An urgent whisper from Kevin broke the spell. Before the silence had a chance to re-form, she pulled herself together. 'I've stopped to see it's safe, of course.' Her voice sounded thin and small in the emptiness.

'Well, is it?' he asked. 'I don't want to make a fuss, but my foot's killing me. These rungs aren't much fun in bare feet.'

'Wait a minute.' Alison twisted round to check behind her, and found to her relief that there actually was something. 'It's all right. It's a hall or something. I've come up beside a wall. Can't see anything else yet. I'm going up.'

She unhooked the lantern from her wrist and put

it down on the floor. Then she climbed the last rungs of the ladder. Mave scrambled after her, creating a minor dust-storm in her eagerness to get off the ladder.

'Be careful!' Kevin's alarmed face appeared in the opening. 'I'm supposed to be—' An explosion of sneezing so violent he looked in danger of falling off the ladder cut him short. With a snort of exasperation, Alison grabbed his arm, and hauled him up. 'Sensitive to house dust,' he finished, on hands and knees at her feet, eyes streaming.

She picked up the lantern. The beam of light revealed ranks of shelves lining the walls. Presumably they went up to the ceiling. No way to tell: the light didn't reach that far. The shelves reminded her of her visit to the storeroom at Westleigh High with Kevin and Mr Dempsey, only these shelves were empty, and over them lay a shroud of dust so deep it must have taken years to settle.

No, not years – she reached out and touched a cautious finger to the edge of the shelf – centuries.

'It's a storeroom.' Kevin, who had come to stand beside her, stated the obvious with his usual fearlessness. He seemed at least to have stopped sneezing. 'And it's empty. Where do we go from here?'

'I don't know,' Alison admitted. Mave winked at

her. Exasperated by her apparent belief that they shared some secret, she added, 'I mean I *really* don't know. What's more, I haven't known for ages. The truth is, I haven't a clue what to do about Plan X.'

'You must have a clue,' Mave insisted. 'You're Zelda.'

'I'm not!'

'You are! You've got to be. There's no one else.'

All at once Alison was aware of having climbed very fast up an enormously long ladder. A split second before her knees gave way, she sat down on the floor.

'It's not true that there's no one else.' Kevin sounded hurt. 'There's me. I sometimes have good ideas. I don't know quite where they come from,' he confessed with characteristic frankness, 'and some of them are a bit strange, but they often work. As a matter of fact—' the two sceptical faces turned in his direction suddenly proved the last straw. 'As a matter of fact, I'm having one now.'

This was a lie. Worse still, it was a flop into the bargain.

'You don't look as though you're having a good idea,' Mave said dispassionately.

Alison sighed and frowned at her fingernails. 'So what is it, then?'

Kevin's mind went blank, but after the last few

days he was expecting that. And he had his own way of dealing with it.

'Why have you shut your eyes?' Mave demanded.

Kevin's eyes flew open. And the first thing he saw looming up through the gloom was—

'The trapdoor!' he exclaimed, inspired. 'We ought to shut it. What if one of us falls down the hole? Or something comes up through it?'

As ideas go, it wasn't a world-beater, but even Mave admitted it made sense. She went to lower the trapdoor into place. And as soon as she did, Alison saw it – what looked like the toe of a shoe poking out from under the shelf against which the door had been leaning.

'Hey! Look!' She advanced with the lamp. 'Just what you need, Kevin. A pair of boots.'

'There!' said Alison bracingly as Kevin laced up the second boot. 'It does fit. And there weren't any spiders.'

'I feel a complete wally. And I look one too.' Kevin looked hopefully from Mave to Alison, waiting for a denial, which didn't come.

The thing about fashions in footwear is, they change. Purple boots with a huge gold star on each toecap might once have been all the rage in Theromantia, but if so, Kevin had a hunch it had been a short one. As for the emerald laces the designer – probably the A.B. who'd left his initials blazed across the heels – had chosen to finish off the outfit, they would have been a lot less disastrous if they hadn't been heavily festooned with silver bells.

'Anyone would look a wally in boots like that,' Alison said with the praiseworthy aim of cheering him up. 'It's not your fault. And you'd look even worse wearing just one of them.' He thanked her stiffly and stood up to the sound of melodious tinkling.

She averted her eyes tactfully. 'Come on, it's time we found our way out. You know, I've been thinking that—'

With an earsplitting *screech*! a cat shot out of the gloom to their right, fur on end, eyes blazing.

Crash! From the same direction came the unmistakable sound of a heavy door slammed shut.

Skid! Two dishevelled figures, barely recognisable as Sep and Fentwick, came pelting into view at a brisk stagger.

Last but not least, *whumf*! An elderly bald stranger in a striped dressing-gown materialised on the floor before them, framed in a rectangle of gold light.

'Yes?' the apparition demanded. 'Repeat the incantation and deliver your question.'

After several seconds – during which Kevin showed little sign of speaking, moving, or breathing

– the stranger let out what could only be called a snuffle of impatience. 'And be quick about it, I'm running a bath.'

Chapter Fifteen

'The boots!' Fentwick pointed a quivering finger. His face was aglow with awe and envy. 'They work! They've conjured up the shade of Alfred Baxtenbrat!'

Sep gulped like someone swallowing a frog. For the second time in his life, a theory of his had proved stunningly right. Given what had followed the first time, he wasn't sure he was ready for such success. And what was Alison doing in the middle of it all – or was she still Zelda? He wasn't sure he knew anything any more, except that he was terribly tired. He swallowed again, and said in tones of foreboding, 'So it appears.'

'What does he mean, "shade"?' Alison muttered, although she had a nasty feeling she knew the answer.

Kevin felt the same. His knees sagged and he turned pale as he answered with resolute cheerfulness, 'I think it means somebody's ghost.'

This statement – greeted by Alison and Mave with dismayed silence – understandably set the seal on Alfred Baxtenbrat's ill-temper. There are few things more galling to a wizard who has just cheated time and space and crossed countless dimensions than to be called a ghost.

'I cannot begin to tell you,' he said tightly, 'how irritating I find this. I go to considerable trouble, not to mention personal expense, to construct a pair of magic boots which will permit the wearer to contact me in a theromantic emergency—'

'*Magic* boots?' Strongly moved, Kevin fixed Alison with a gaze of burning reproach. 'You told me to put them on. I didn't want to. That's you all over: you just don't think. And now look!'

'How was I to know?' A loud hiss cut the argument short.

'If I may continue? Generously overlooking the many differences between us, I place these priceless boots at the disposal of the Wizards' Council for use

in future generations. I have the forethought to draw up a contract specifying the conditions in which they are to be preserved. I have this document signed, sealed and witnessed by eighty-seven of my so-called professional colleagues. And what happens?'

Fentwick, who had been giving the visitor an eagle-eyed inspection, took advantage of this rhetorical pause to lean forward and give him a brisk tap on the head.

The response was a hiss, and a furious swat of the hand as Fentwick bobbed out of reach. 'Extraordinary,' the professor observed to Similon, feigning an unconcern he was far from feeling. (The ghost's head was solid – solid as a hard-boiled egg! What sort of shade was this?) 'He feels surprisingly real. Try it yourself.'

Similon uttered a mild bleating noise. Alison recognised it as a sign of severe unease. 'I don't think that would be wise,' he said, backing away. 'He doesn't seem to like people touching him. We don't want him to disappear.'

'He couldn't if he wanted to!' Fentwick was guessing wildly, but guessing right. 'He's been summoned. He can't go till young what's-his-face lets him.'

'The name's Kevin,' said Kevin with dignity.

He might have saved his breath. The full

possibilities of the situation had begun to dawn on the professor. An expression of unholy glee spread across his face. 'We can tell the old windbag anything we newting well like! By Logios, I hardly know where to start.'

Similon's whinny indicated that he had made the transition from unease to panic. 'Don't!' He clapped a hand over Fentwick's mouth. 'This isn't a game, remember? It's our last chance. Before you go calling him names, let's try to put things right.'

This was so obviously sound advice that Fentwick's struggles ceased. Edging closer to Kevin – as she said later, it wasn't that he was any more use than Sep or Fentwick, just that he seemed a bit saner – Alison felt a hand slip into hers; Mave following her like a shadow.

'I will tell you what happens,' Baxtenbrat continued, oblivious to the fact that no one was asking. 'Nothing! For one hundred and thirty-nine years nobody bothers to contact me! And when at last the summons comes, what do I find?' He took a deep breath. Every part of his body, from his ears down to the soles of his neat small feet, seemed to swell with outrage. 'I find that my boots, these priceless bequests, have been left unguarded in an abandoned storeroom, at the mercy of any passing vagabond. One such picks them up, has the temerity to put them on, and chooses to disrupt my evening ablutions for nothing more than his own amusement! And now he appears to be ignorant of the correct incantation! I am displeased.' Alfred Baxtenbrat's eyes glittered, and his nostrils were pinched. Anyone could see he was telling the truth. 'I am seriously displeased.'

Fentwick took advantage of a lapse of attention on Similon's part to push his hand away. 'Oh, put a frog in it! This *is* a theromantic emergency. Small wonder no one wanted to talk to you for a century if you carry on like this.'

Something in the visitor's eyes made him fall back a step, despite himself. Baxtenbrat gave an unpleasant smile as he registered the victory. 'I see no boots on your feet,' he observed thinly. He did the swelling trick again. 'Unbelievers mock me at their peril! As for you, boy—' His gaze swung round to transfix Kevin, who was only still there because he was too embarrassed to draw attention to himself by making a run for it. 'My boots were not made for fools like you. Remove them instantly, and set me free.'

In the circumstances, this struck Kevin as an excellent idea. He bent down. At one and the same moment, both wizards spotted the danger.

'No!' cried Similon. 'He'll vanish!'

'Don't!' bellowed Fentwick. 'Not till we ask him!'

Their cries blended to a meaningless blur, which

Kevin felt free to ignore. The sooner the boots were off, the sooner the terrifying, bald phantom could go back to whatever dimension he had come from. It couldn't be a moment too soon for Kevin. Making the most of the lull as both wizards drew breath, he tugged hastily at the laces.

'Don't!' shrieked Similon.

'No!' yelled Fentwick.

'Listen to them!' shouted Alison.

'Stop, you stupid Grorkling!' screamed Mave, backing her up.

Good grief! It was as bad as trying to get changed for football with Mr Davis peeping his whistle – and, from Kevin's point of view, the result was much the same.

He sighed, and looked up. 'Bit of a problem, actually,' he said, resigned. 'Can't take them off. There's a knot.'

'Wizards everywhere – that's how it was, that's how it will be. The time will come,' said Catterat broodingly, 'when we will emerge from our caves, and return in triumph to our rightful home.'

Huddled speechless and motionless on the far side of the cave where they had taken shelter when the tablecloth dumped them, Strepticon felt less hopeful. His brain told him he was lucky to be alive, but his body wasn't listening. The firelight hurt his eyes, and the least tilt of his head was torture. He felt the bump above his right ear with a cautious finger.

'You're groaning again,' Catterat said disapprovingly.

'I can't help it, Catters.'

'Then groan quietly. And I thought I had made it clear that you are not to call me that.'

A tear slid down Strepticon's cheek. What a wizard needed at a time like this was a friend, someone who would speak soft words of sympathy and fetch glasses of fizzy medicine. Instead of which, he had Catterat, and no prospect of anything to eat or drink except whatever his companion was brewing up in a folding saucepan.

What sort of wizard carried a folding saucepan about with him, for the love of Logios? And how could he possibly expect any sane person to eat the stuff he cooked?

He'd rather die.

The way his head felt, he was going to die anyway.

In his little room in the east wing of the castle, there was a chest beside the bed. Inside, nestling between an elderly dragon's claw and a rolled map depicting the travels of Habbakuk the Navigator, was a pill-box. Inside that were four tablets of crushed frumenswort. Two of these, according to his great-aunt Rubigon, were enough to cure the sort of mild headache brought about by poring over council accounts.

Oh, to have those tablets now, all four of them!

He bit back another groan as a pang like a red-hot poker stabbed him through the right eye. In the name of every wizard that had ever wielded a thaumoflux, better the wolves than put up with this.

He dragged himself to his feet and stood, swaying gently, uncertain whether or not to be sick.

Catterat glanced up from the saucepan with a frown. 'You would be wise to keep still. You do not appear to be well.'

'I have to get to the castle, Catters – I mean, Catterat.'

'You can't. What's more, I forbid you to try. We are the only two senior wizards who are both alive and in any sense fit to function. The future of the profession rests with us.'

'What about Charufex?' Strepticon cried unwisely. He clutched his head as a wave of molten fire rolled across his skull. 'You said he got away. What about Fentwick, and young Similon?'

A flush of anger drew blood to Catterat's cheeks. 'Similon! Logios help us if the fate of wizardry depends on him. He is nothing less than a disaster waiting to happen! For all we know, Fentwick is dead; with our crystals melted, we have no way of knowing. As for Charufex – I trust he will enjoy a long and happy life as an anteater, since if I ever encounter him again as a wizard, I shall have no hesitation in ordering his arrest. He was told, he was expressly ordered, *not* to use magic, yet the first time he finds himself face to face with a two-headed, fire-breathing monster the size of a banqueting hall, he tries to do just that. Incomprehensible!'

Summoning all his strength, Strepticon managed a step towards the cave entrance. 'If I don't take something for this headache, I'll die. It's as simple as that. If—' he pressed his lips together and took another wobbly step '— if I don't come back . . .'

'Yes?' Catterat said thinly after a distressing interval.

'Tell them, Catters,' said Strepticon faintly, 'tell everyone: never mix bats-blood and triple-strength elixir. It's a bad idea. Goodbye.'

His departure from the cave was unsteady, and brief. Ten seconds later he was back, miraculously restored to working order.

Terror can do that, even to a wizard.

'Catters,' he whispered, eyes wide with horror. 'It's too late. The castle – it's . . . it's burning!'

Kevin's bootlaces were tied in a knot he'd invented himself. It was a good knot, with the minor drawback that you had to be careful undoing it. One hasty tug and it turned into a double-limpet with severe complications. The boots were on Kevin's feet, and there they were going to stay until someone cut him out of them.

Assuming that enchanted laces could be cut. If not . . .

'I could be stuck in them for ever!' Kevin said, showing no sign of being prepared to look on the bright side. 'And stuck with him too!'

Fentwick nodded briskly. Similon gave a tortured, sympathetic twitch, which came to the same thing. Kevin's dwindling store of optimism vanished in a puff of smoke as he glimpsed a future in which Alfred Baxtenbrat marched at his side, hissing audibly at every step.

'Terrific!' he said wanly.

'Oh for goodness' sake!' For the past five minutes, Alison had been biting her tongue. Even she could see that the less you argued with two live wizards and one dead one, the greater chance you had of staying alive and more or less recognisable. Her patience had limits, though. 'Stop going on about it, you three. Kevin's got the stupid boots on. Why doesn't one of you tell him the wretched incantation and get it over with. Then, even if he,' she pointed at Baxtenbrat, seething like a saucepan on too high a heat, 'doesn't have the answer, we can push off home. I'm tired, really tired,' she finished with sudden passion, 'of dust and gloom and cobwebs. And stupid arguments, from people –' she glared at them, arms akimbo '– who should know better.'

'Well?' growled Fentwick, taking his embarrassment out on Similon. 'How much longer are you going to funk it? Use the newting incantation, before we die of a surfeit of frogs and boredom.' He sneezed. 'It's like an oven in here. Why can't children have the sense to keep still and not go kicking up dust?'

On the point of denying indignantly that she had been responsible for kicking up anything, Alison stopped dead.

Fentwick was right. Something had stirred up the dust: great clouds of it were rising in swirls from the wooden floorboards.

Only it wasn't dust.

It was smoke.

The destruction of a castle is a terrible thing.

Stone won't burn, but only the outer walls were made of stone. Inside was a patchwork of materials as old as the centuries, which fire can unpick in minutes. Wood smoulders and bursts into bright flowers of flame. Tapestries spark, ignite, crumble. Iron melts. The stone itself seems to buckle and curl inwards as the fire takes hold.

Wolves flee, and all living creatures flee with

209

them – except for one. The few townsfolk brave enough to peer through a crack in their shutters at the blazing hillside above Stolk saw a monstrous shadow circling the blaze; the thelamungus, revelling in the heat and the downfall of his ancient foes.

After ten minutes, the townsfolk closed their shutters and went to bed. The castle was burning, and no one was particularly sorry. Wizards, once a source of mild entertainment, had become a luxury people couldn't afford.

Let the castle vanish, and the wizards with it.

Who cares?

'*Cargill fitzdod y tzenkil hamma*,' croaked Kevin. He looked hopefully at Baxtenbrat.

For the second time the wizard coughed and shook his head. He looked as if he felt the heat and smoke as much as the rest of them, but it didn't seem to make a difference. Unless Kevin used exactly the right incantation, faultlessly pronounced in Universal, Alfred Baxtenbrat was not going to give them the time of day, let alone reveal how to reverse Similon's barrier or leave the burning castle.

'Tell us what we want to know, worm!' Fentwick raged as he struggled to break out of the half nelson Similon had been forced to apply to keep his supervisor from throttling their only hope. 'You'll die like us if you don't!'

'I'll last longer than you, unbeliever,' Baxtenbrat gasped.

'Not if I get hold of you, you won't.' Fentwick's body heaved as he tried to shake Similon off. 'Stop interfering! I'll give him newting incantation!'

Clinging to Fentwick with stringy desperation, Similon urged Kevin to try reciting the incantation again. 'In a different order. And this time, sound as if you mean it. I can't hold him much longer.'

'*Cargill y fitzdod hamma, tzenkil*!' Kevin cried with as much passionate sincerity as he could muster. Given that he didn't have a clue what it meant and was in imminent danger of going up in smoke, he felt he wasn't doing badly. '*Hamma y cargill fitzdod tzenkil*!' Another shake of the head. 'I can't take much more of this.'

It looked increasingly as if nobody could, including the cat. The smoke swirled up on every side in thick black clouds, and when Alison allowed herself to look down, she could see a bright glow beneath the cracks in the floorboards. Even if she kept her eyes fixed on Kevin, and both arms tight round Mave, she could still hear the fire roaring its way through the floor below. What Zelda would have done in these circumstances was an interesting question, but one Alison was in no position to

211

answer. Unfortunately, nothing *she* could think of was any use at all.

The ladder had melted.

The corridor outside the storeroom was already alight. Only the heavy door was keeping the fire at bay, and that had already begun to smoulder. They had minutes left before the flames broke through. Even Baxtenbrat was looking at Kevin now as if, too stubborn to tell him what he was supposed to say, he was none the less willing him desperately to get it right.

'Again!' Similon let go of Fentwick from sheer exhaustion. His voice had frayed to a hoarse thread. 'Keep trying!'

'*Hamma cargill y tzenkil fitzdod. Fitzdod y hamma tzenkil cargill.*' How many more ways to combine the words could there possibly be? '*Y tzenkil hamma fitzdod cargill.*' Kevin shouted in despair.

'That's it!' yelled Fentwick and Similon simultaneously. At exactly the same moment, Alfred Baxtenbrat spat out three soft words.

And vanished.

'It is the end, the end,' Catterat chanted in a grim, high wail. Rain had begun to fall, but the drops made no impression on the flames. There were tears on his cheeks.

'The end,' echoed Strepticon dutifully, trying not

to dwell on the thought that the end of this particular ritual was going to be a relief. To a wizard long past his prime, skipping about on a hillside with an aching head, a churning stomach, a grazed elbow, and the beginnings of a sore throat, even the cave had begun to seem like home – yet he too wept, silently and without concealment.

'The castle is Theromantia.' Stooping, Catterat pressed his right hand to the ground. 'Theromantia is the castle.' He stood up, and pressed the muddy palm to his cheeks and forehead. Then he looked at Strepticon, who followed suit.

'The castle is doomed. Theromantia is doomed.' Catterat's voice was clear and steady. 'The lexifer is torn, the thaumuflux broken. We will die with the castle.' He looked again at Strepticon.

There was a pause, while Strepticon swallowed. 'Die with the castle? You're speaking metaphorically, aren't you?'

'We will die with the castle. That is what the ritual dictates.'

'But not actually die, surely?' Shocked to the core, Strepticon scanned the Chief Wizard's features with disbelief. The grim face told him nothing. 'But we're the last of the wizards!' Strepticon cried desperately. 'If we die, who's going to come after us? It doesn't make sense!'

'The directions are quite specific. A Chief Wizard

goes down with his castle. The council accompanies him.' There was a mighty crack as part of the blazing structure collapsed. A fountain of sparks exploded into the sky. For a moment Catterat's face was lit from above by the lurid light. Then a huge shadow swooped, blotting it out.

Strepticon looked up and gave a scream of terror. 'Thelamungus! Run, Catters!'

A hand seized the tail of his cloak. With a wail of despair, Strepticon reeled and fell. 'We die with the castle,' said Catterat, bitter and implacable. 'There is no reference to metaphor.'

The crack seemed faint and far away, but it broke the spell of shocked silence that had seized them all.

'That's it,' Fentwick said in an odd, flat voice. 'I didn't think Baxtenbrat could go without answering. But he has. That's it,' he said again, as if it was of prime importance to get this straight. 'We're done for.'

Before his words could sink in, Alison said in an uncertain voice, 'Rub it out.'

No one paid attention. 'We've got two minutes, I should think.' Fentwick looked across at Similon, bushy eyebrows raised, one professional consulting another.

'Two and a quarter. This simply cannot happen!'

Similon said in the grip of unprofessional anguish. 'It's against all the rules to go without giving us an answer. It isn't fair!'

'Rub it out!' Alison said, louder. Over the roar of the flames she could hear her own heart thudding. 'That's what he said. I heard him. That must be the answer.' And a fat lot of good it did them, she thought, still curiously calm.

'Rub what out?' Fentwick yelled, voicing her thoughts. 'What did the old coot mean, for the love of Logios? Has one of you idiots been frogging around with a pencil?'

'No!'

'Because if you have . . .'

Kevin became aware that something strange was happening. The angry voices faded, as if an invisible hand had adjusted a sound control inside his head. In the sudden silence three words swam up before his eyes, typed in huge, bold letters, like a film title on a giant screen:

pencil
circle
map

Very deliberately, in case a sudden movement should break the spell and cause a disaster, Kevin reached into his pocket and pulled out the map.

It was spooky, being able to see someone scream and not hear it.

Fentwick snatched the map, beard wagging nineteen to the dozen. Similon, gabbling wildly, rummaged madly through his pockets, and came up with a pencil-stub, crowned with an eraser.

It was as good as a play, Kevin thought placidly. How long until the final curtain? Forty seconds? Thirty?

Less than that, if the desperate way Sep wielded the eraser was any indication. It was a wonder he didn't rub right through the paper . . . What acting! The man deserved an Oscar!

Twenty seconds, that would be all they had left now. Ten, nine, eight, seven—

'Brace youselves!' Fentwick's bellow jolted Kevin out of his trance. 'He's almost there! It's anybody's guess what happens next!'

Chapter Sixteen

They were in Sep's room, the three of them, sprawled on the floor in a complicated tangle.

Alison let go of Kevin's leg and sat up hurriedly. The movement dislodged something from her sleeve, which fell on to the carpet. She picked it up, gave a cry, and dropped it again as she recognised what it was: an ember of charred wood, still hot.

Sep, with unexpected presence of mind, reached for a volume of Logios and thwacked it down on the smouldering fragment. Wisps of smoke still drifted up from his hair in curly tendrils, she noticed with a second shock. And Kevin!

'Ruined,' he said, examining the biggest hole in his grey sweater. 'I can't wait to show Mum. She's been going on at me for years to let myself go. Now she'll think I have. Play my cards right and she'll double my clothes allowance.' He stood up, rather unsteady, saw what was on his feet, and sat down again, fast. 'I'm not going anywhere in these,' he said with great firmness, 'not even to give Mum a shock.' He looked pleadingly at Alison. 'Could you find me a knife?'

'There should be a pair of scissors somewhere. Wait a minute.' Sep rose to his feet and staggered across the room. The table was still covered with its sea of papers. He dived in among them with both hands.

'You and your knots!' Alison gave one of Kevin's boots a friendly nudge with her foot. 'I suppose they saved us, really. If it hadn't been for them, you'd have taken the boots off, and if you'd done that, Baxtenbrat would have vanished, and – Kevin! what on earth is the matter?'

Kevin was staring at the space under Sep's bed. 'There's something under there. I can see its eyes watching me. Probably nothing important,' he said with airy unconcern. 'Probably just one of his familiars. He'd have familiars, wouldn't he? A pocket-sized dragon, a vampire gerbil, something along those lines. Uh-oh, it's coming out.'

'For the love of Logios,' Alison said as a black shape emerged from under the bedsprings. 'It's only the cat! Sep—' she took a step towards the table and immediately tripped over a pile of books. 'You can't keep a cat up here,' she said crossly from the carpet. 'And you absolutely *have* to tidy up.'

'A cat?' Behind her, Kevin's voice sounded peculiar. When Alison scrambled up she saw why.

The cat was no longer a cat, or any other identifiable creature, but a pillar of movement and shadow, light and darkness mixed. 'Sep!' she screeched. 'You can't keep *that* in here either. Make it go away!'

'What?' Sep continued to flap randomly at his papers. He didn't even turn round. 'Hang on.'

'SEP!'

'There's no need to get worked up.' The pillar of shadow resolved itself suddenly into a girl of much the same age as Alison. 'I won't be staying. I've got the Organisation to rebuild, a revolution to arrange, and a sister to look after. Logios knows what she'll get up to if I leave her alone. She hasn't got over the fire yet. You seem to have had a better home-coming than we did. At least your home's still standing.' The girl turned her tawny eyes on Alison and held out a hand. 'Thanks for looking after Mave, by the way. You weren't much good, but you tried. I appreciate that.'

'Thank you,' said Alison crossly. 'I take it you're Zelda?'

'Who else?' said the girl calmly. 'I was on a fact-finding mission here when that genius by the window –' she nodded at Similon '– upset everything. With the barrier giving out interference, I couldn't get back. If it hadn't been for him –' she turned her direct gaze towards Kevin, who was goggling at her with what Alison considered a ridiculous degree of fascination '– I'd be stuck a cat for ever. You have my undying gratitude,' she said, reaching down a slender, muscular hand.

Mumbling incoherently, Kevin made the mistake of taking it. He found himself hauled to his feet, gazing into the tawny eyes at unnervingly close quarters.

'I like a wimp who knows he's a wimp,' she said, carrying out a swift appraisal. 'Most men make the mistake of pretending. I find self-knowledge a devastatingly attractive quality.' Her lips were so close to Kevin's cheek that he could feel her breath fan his cheek. He blushed and tried to retreat. 'Come to Theromantia, my little Grorkling,' she whispered, pulling him closer without visible effort, 'and I'll teach you my secrets.'

'I beg your pardon!' Alison slipped her arm through Kevin's and, without knowing quite how she managed it, yanked him out of reach.

Kevin blushed again, this time with surprise. 'Yes,' he said to cover his confusion, 'and I've got to see Mum and Dad. They'll be wondering where I've been. At least, I hope they will.'

'Of course they'll have been wondering.' While Alison said these bracing words, she continued to watch Zelda like a hawk. The nerve of some people . . . 'Everyone will. We'll be the talk of Axborough.'

'I don't know. When I went on a French exchange last year, I was gone two weeks and nobody noticed. All I found when I came home was a note from Mum pinned on the door asking when I was going to clean out the hamster. So I'm not banking on anything. Still, I've had enough of Theromantia for the moment,' he said politely, addressing Zelda. 'It's been very nice meeting you, and if I ever go back again, I'll certainly look you up.'

'Don't hold your breath,' growled Alison as the cat-girl thinned, rippled and vanished. Only when she was quite sure they had the room to themselves once more did she let go of Kevin's arm and round on Similon.

'Don't help or anything, will you?' she demanded. 'I mean, she practically kidnapped him under your very nose, and all you seem to care about is your books and papers. Have you found the scissors yet, or haven't you?'

'Something's wrong with him,' said Kevin, showing once again that he could be unexpectedly perceptive.

Similon stood frozen, both hands braced against the tabletop, as if their support was all that kept him from collapsing. It was not, Alison and Kevin discovered when they went to see what was wrong, a pair of scissors that had brought on his paralysis.

It was the map. It lay, unfolded to its fullest extent on the table, as it had been on the afternoon when Sep had drawn the circle.

It was the map, and it wasn't. Alison stared at it. It wasn't what she saw that bewildered her so much as what all the fuss was about. Surely by now Sep, of all wizards, should be used to the quirks of reality adjustment?

'OK, it's turned into a map of Stolk,' she said, pointing at the title, 'in the realm of Theromantia. I don't see the problem, Sep.' His face was pinched and grey with shock. 'It's been reality adjusted, that's all. We know all about that. It doesn't mean anything.' She looked across at Kevin, and added more dubiously, 'Does it?'

Kevin's eyes were on another part of the map, the key. He cleared his throat and tapped an official-looking seal with his finger.

Alison looked again. 'What? Oh!' For some reason there was a lump in her throat. 'I was wrong, Sep, it does mean something. It must!'

The official seal announced that the map had been drawn on the forty-ninth day of the month of Rabilhar on the instructions of Septimus Similon, to celebrate his election as Chief Wizard.

'Do you really have to go?' Alison asked against her better judgement, ignoring the small inner voice that asked if she seriously wanted to have the Chief Wizard of Theromantia living one floor above her bedroom. 'If it's the tidying up you're worried about, we'll help. And I promise I won't tell Mum you're to blame for everything. Even though you were. Joke,' she said hastily, dodging Kevin's elbow. 'I mean, the castle's burned to the ground. Most of the other wizards are anteaters. Who will you have to boss about?'

'What she's trying to ask,' interrupted Kevin, 'is what there is to go back to?'

'There may not be a great deal. But I'm Chief Wizard,' Similon said simply. 'I don't know how or why, but somehow that is what's happened, and I have the feeling it's the last reality adjustment there's going to be. My place is at home, trying to sort things out. You'll send my stuff on later, won't you?'

She cast a blank look round at the chaos of the attic. 'How? Do they have intergalactic furniture removals? And who's going to pack it up?'

'I'll book a special collection. They'll come with boxes and everything. I'll ring in about ten days to let you know the date.'

'Ring? From Theromantia?'

'Don't worry. I'll have a phone, and fax, and all sorts of things now I'm Chief Wizard. I won't have to reverse charges.'

Alison didn't have the heart to say that wasn't what she meant. She and Kevin watched the wizard stuff a handful of belongings into a carrier bag, and with a mixture of relief and sadness, accompanied him down the stairs.

'Do you want to be Chief Wizard?' Kevin asked to fill the pause as they hovered by the front door, wondering whether to shake hands or hug.

Sep gave a painful smile. 'I used to. There was a time when I dreamed of it. But after what's happened . . .' He shook his head. 'I'll try to make a good job of it. That's all.'

'You couldn't make a worse job than Catterat,' said Alison with less truth than loyalty.

Similon shook his head. 'I wouldn't say that. He had a lot to cope with. I wonder what became of him?'

'I couldn't care less,' Alison said fiercely. 'It's you we care about.'

A peculiar look came over Similon's face. 'No

one's ever said that to me before. Excuse me – if I don't leave, I may cry, and that would make it even harder to be Chief Wizard. I don't suppose I could trouble you for the loan of fifty pence for the bus?'

'I have some money.' By a heroic effort, Kevin managed not to catch Alison's eye as he rummaged in his pocket. However, as he handed over a one-pound coin, he couldn't resist asking, 'You're catching a bus? To Theromantia?'

'Yes. Or rather, no.' Sep did his imitation of an anguished sheep. 'I can't say any more – it's against the Wizard's Code, and I have to set a good example. Goodbye, Kevin. Goodbye, Alison.' He shook them each solemnly by the hand, then surprised everyone, most of all himself, by dropping the carrier bag and hugging them tight. As he let Alison go he said in a low voice, 'If you get the chance, please tell your mother—?'

He broke off. To her chagrin, Alison found she was close to crying. 'Tell her what, Sep?' She gave a hearty sniff. 'If it's that stain on the carpet—'

He silenced her by squeezing both her hands painfully in his. 'Just tell her. From me. I always meant to mention it. Goodbye!'

He set off down the road at an anguished trot. As he passed the next house, he turned one last time. His last words floated back to them on the wind,

anxious and insubstantial, the essence of Septimus
Similon:

'And take care of the anteaters. Goodbye . . .'

Alison and Kevin stood watching until he had
hurried out of sight. A car drew up to the pavement
and a woman got out. Kevin withdrew tactfully
inside while Alison sped down the steps and flung
both arms round her mother. 'Mum! I'm back! I
hope you weren't too worried.'

'Worried?' After one hearty squeeze, her mother
let her go and went to open the boot of the car.
'On a school trip? With Mr Dempsey in charge? –
Take this bag, darling. And mind, it's heavy – Why
should I be worried? Of course, a telephone call
would have been nice, or a postcard, and the school
secretary sounded quite vague when I asked for the
itinerary, but I was never in the least worried about
you.'

Her mother headed up the steps. Alison stayed
where she was, in a state of shock.

She hadn't been worried?

People hadn't even missed her?

All the time she and Kevin had been dodging
fanatical wizards and two-headed fire-breathing
monsters, they were supposed to have been on some
sort of school trip?

This was reality adjustment on a totally new scale.

Why, she wondered, as she went slowly inside, had it never crossed her mind that the same process had been at work on both sides of the barrier? The same need to knit up loose ends, to account for what was totally unaccountable . . .

She stuck her head into the kitchen. Kevin was helping unpack groceries.

'Hmm! So you're Kevin, are you?' Mrs Braythwayte said as Alison opened the door. Her mother spoke with noticeable frostiness. 'I may as well tell you that Janice mentioned your name when she popped in yesterday evening.'

'Did she?' Kevin sounded startled, but he had no chance to say, Janice who?

Mrs Braythwayte pounced on a box of cereal like a cat on a rat. 'You're some sort of martial arts expert, am I right? And I hear there was an incident with Mr Davis after football on Tuesday?'

'Well, actually, I wasn't there on—'

'An accident was what Janice said, but it didn't sound like an accident to me. A bicycle chain is a very dangerous thing, in thoughtless hands. Furthermore, Kevin Grork—'

Kevin had to show her his library card to persuade her she'd got the wrong person. Even then, she didn't seem totally convinced. All things considered, it seemed best to go home.

Mrs Braythwayte was unmoved by Alison's

reproaches, largely because she was so used to them. 'You can't be too careful,' she said peering at a Sell By date with suspicion. 'Things have been happening while you were away. I'm serious, Alison. You would not believe half of them.'

'Try me.' Alison said. 'I've had a lot of practice lately.'

'It's not just the business with Kevin Grork and Mr Davis. While Mr Dempsey was away, the school drafted in a supply teacher – Zachariah Zlot, or some weird name like that. For some inexplicable reason, they made him Acting Head, and he only went and tried to change the whole syllabus. You can imagine the fuss. The parents were up in arms, naturally, what with GCSEs less than six months away. Children started refusing to go to school – he had some very strange ideas on discipline, apparently, not to mention the frogs. Then this afternoon the school secretary Mrs Sandall rang up to say the Head was back – in a terrible state, according to her. Remind me to ask you why later – and that Zlot had up and vanished, taking the petty cash with him. Then she rang up the Department, and they didn't know anything about him! He was a complete imposter! So don't talk to me about taking people on trust. These days, you can't be too careful. Now,' she slammed the fridge shut with an air of triumph, 'tell me all about what you've been up to on this trip of yours.'

So Alison did exactly that.

Similon stood facing the ruins of Stolk Castle. Ranged around him was a semicircle of anteaters and bedraggled wizards. The air smelled of rain and woodsmoke.

The new Chief Wizard was tired, wet, and at a loss for words. He was glad to have Fentwick at his side, his public-relations aide and newly-appointed speech-writer. He cleared his throat and waited nervously for his cue.

'The castle is fallen,' hissed a voice in his left ear.

'I think they can see that,' Similon answered without moving his lips.

'It's the last Appendix in the Collected Works, you nincompoop: *Whatte to saye when ye experienfe a fetback*. Say it! It absolutely never fails.'

Similon cleared his throat again and said in a low, hesitant voice, 'The castle is fallen.'

'What did he say?' demanded a wizard with a long white beard and an ear-trumpet, at one end of the row.

'He said, "The castle is fallen," cloth-ears,' his neighbour reported with wizardly courtesy.

'I would have thought that was perfectly obvious,' an anteater observed in a mournful voice. 'He's not very good, is he?'

'Catterat did it better.'

'Don't pay any attention to them,' Fentwick said loudly, glaring in the ear-trumpet's direction. 'They're jealous. Now say, "The castle will rise again." '

Similon stared at him in stupefaction.

'Go on, say it!'

'But it isn't true! I mean, look at it! There's nothing left! Oh very well, if you're sure I have to.'

'I am. And try not to mutter. They'll think you've been hitting the elixir.'

The Chief Wizard took a deep breath and lifted his head. 'The castle will rise again,' he announced in what a reporter from the *Stolk Echo* later described as ringing tones. 'Or if it doesn't,' he added cautiously, 'we'll ... we'll ... we'll build a substitute! Yes, that's what we'll do!' He began to warm to his theme. 'A castle for the future! A detached multi-purpose structure with bay windows and pebbledash rendering! A five-hundred-seater lecture suite—'

'A thermostatically-controlled froggery!' Fentwick cried, visited with sudden inspiration. Others around him caught the spark. One by one, they rose to give voice to their own dreams.

'An indoor aeriferium!'

'An all-weather carpet pad!'

'An electronically-guided crystal!'

Tears rose to Similon's eyes as the tumult mounted. When it was possible to make his voice heard, he cried: 'I, your Chief Wizard, give you my pledge! I will lead you into the twenty-first century. Stolk Castle is fallen! Stolk Castle will rise again! The wizards are back!'

THE BRUGAN

Stephen Moore

Ugly. Smelly. And a vile shade of green. That's the Brugan. And when he comes crashing into Sarah Lemming's life, she just knows the world will never be the same again. It's not that he *means* to be evil, it's just that his mischief is more dangerous, more powerful, more deadly than anyone could have imagined . . .

THE LAMMAS FIELD

Catherine Fisher

Far away, at the edge of his hearing, was a low thudding. It beat like his heart, but a long way off. It was a beat in the ground and in his head, and even the cobwebs on the window vibrated with the deep thud of it. And suddenly, between one beat and another, he saw it come, as if it rode out of nowhere, over the surface of the lake and on to the dark grass: a white horse gleaming in the moonlight, tiny silver bells on its harness chinking in the warm air, and someone on its back . . .

She comes from nowhere to the Lammas Fair. She brings the gift of music, and for Mick music is life. But her gift carries a price – and a choice more terrible than any Mick could ever dream of . . .

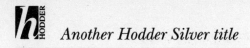

THE BURNING

Judy Allen

To Jan and Kate the changes are gradual but disturbing. An attic opened after years left sealed. A stranger seeking answers to family mysteries. A bonfire kindling on a village green that bears the scars of a terrible fire decades ago. But below the surface of their village, something has beguns its search – for somewhere to feed and grow, for someone to embrace and use its slumbering power . . .

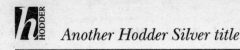

LAW OF THE WOLF TOWER
Shortlisted for the Guardian Children's
Fiction Award

Tanith Lee

'A feast for fans of fantasy. For those long
winter nights by the fire, this will make
compulsive reading' *The Bookseller*

Orphan-slave Claidi knows only the mindless
rituals and cruelties of the House and the
Garden, where ruling families wallow in lavish
extravagance. Then a golden stranger promises
freedom if she will journey with him through
the savage Waste. Mad tribes and strange cities,
enemies and friends where she least expects
them, above all the Wolf Tower that broods
over the grim stone city of her destiny: nothing
– and no one – is as it seems.

If she is to survive, Claidi must learn fast
– hone her wits, sharpen her instinct for
danger . . . Freedom demands that she confront
the Law – once and for all . . .